HOW I
BECAME
A DOG
CALLED
MIDNIGHT

Other books by Ben Miller

The Night I Met Father Christmas

The Boy Who Made the World Disappear

The Day I Fell Into a Fairytale

Diary of a Christmas Elf — *coming soon*!

BEN MILLER

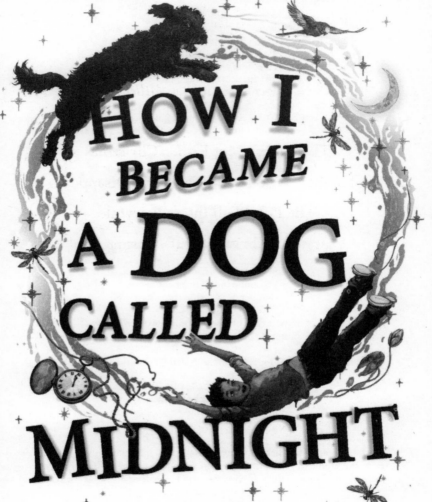

HOW I BECAME A DOG CALLED MIDNIGHT

Illustrated by
Daniela Jaglenka Terrazzini

SIMON & SCHUSTER

First published in Great Britain in 2021 by Simon & Schuster UK Ltd

1 3 5 7 9 10 8 6 4 2

Simon & Schuster UK Ltd
1st Floor, 222 Gray's Inn Road
London
WC1X 8HB

www.simonandschuster.co.uk
www.simonandschuster.com.au
www.simonandschuster.co.in

Simon & Schuster Australia, Sydney
Simon & Schuster India, New Delhi

A CIP catalogue record for this book is available from the British Library.

HB ISBN 978-1-4711-9248-7
PB ISBN 978-1-4711-9246-3
eBook ISBN 978-1-4711-9247-0
eAudio ISBN: 978-1-3985-0017-4

Printed and bound by CPI Group (UK) Ltd, Croydon, CR0 4YY

MIX
Paper from
responsible sources
FSC® C020471

For Ruby and Angus

CHAPTER ONE

'George? I've got a surprise for you.'

It was his mum's voice, soft and low. George looked up to see her and his dad, bathed in light.

'Close your eyes and hold out your hands.'

Doing as he was told, he felt the prick of tiny paws and the heat of an animal's body.

'You can look now.'

A puppy! A miniature, pink-nosed puppy with

pink ears, white fur and huge blue eyes!

'She's an albino chihuahua', said his dad. 'Twelve weeks old and she's looking for a new home.'

George blinked in disbelief. He'd wanted a puppy for ever! For a moment he was so excited he forgot to breathe.

'Can we keep her?' he asked.

'She's yours, George.' His mum smiled. 'What are you going to call her?'

'Snowball,' he said instantly.

Taking care not to drop her, George raised one thumb and stroked the back of the puppy's tiny head. She seemed to like it. 'Hello, Snowball,' he whispered.

Snowball licked his thumbnail.

As the three of them watched, teeny-tiny Snowball sat up tall, closed her eyes, tipped back her head and let out an ENORMOUS, quite definitely terrifying HOWL!

George woke with a start and sat upright in bed, heart thumping.

CHAPTER TWO

George had dreamed about the puppy again; the one his mum had given him just before she died. It was a dream that started with him feeling happy and secure, and ended with him feeling sad and alone, because his mum wasn't here any more.

The fact that he and his dad had to give Snowball away soon afterwards made him even sadder.

The howl, though. That was a new twist.

George took a deep breath, plumped his pillow, and tried to settle back down. Which was when he heard it again.

A BONE-CHILLING, FULL-THROATED HOWL, echoing off into the night!

Something was out there, in the woods that surrounded the cottage. *But what was it?*

Eyes wide, George slid off the bed, crept to the window, and pulled back the curtain. A large moon hung beyond the whispering trees. He checked the time on his bedside clock. It was almost midnight!

It had *sounded* like a wolf. But there were no wolves in England, were there?

His dad would know what to do. George slipped on his dressing gown and opened his bedroom door.

The lights were on – his father was still up!

'Dad?'

5

The long-legged figure by the wood burner didn't move. George tiptoed closer. His dad was fast asleep in his favourite armchair, an old book in his lap, head tipped back and snoring. He was still in his work clothes; his short dark hair was tousled and a half-eaten cheese toastie sat beside him.

Outside in the woods, the creature howled again!

Gabe snuffled but didn't wake. That made George's mind up: he would go and investigate himself. Sliding into his big coat, he twisted his bare feet into his wellies. With one last glance at his sleeping father, he was outside.

His eyes took a few seconds to adjust to the darkness as he made a few clumsy steps off the stony path into the trees. Then he froze. Somewhere up ahead, something was moving.

It was big and blundering, crashing through

shrubs and ripping brambles. A deer, maybe, or a badger? George felt his chest tighten. No wild animal moved like that, not normally. Not unless it was injured. And injured animals could be dangerous . . .

The noises stopped. The creature had sensed him. For a heart-stopping moment, their two spirits locked together in the stillness of the woods.

Then it burst out of the bushes, lurching towards him!

George took flight, racing for the lights of the cottage, but the creature was fast – much too fast. He took a few more steps before a heavy weight struck him between his shoulder blades, knocking him face down into the mud!

What was coming next? Teeth? Claws? George rolled into a ball, shielding his head with his hands. But all that came was a nose. A huge, wet nose, sniffing his neck, his armpits, and under his jumper. Then a tongue. A colossal, slobbering tongue, wiping him down like a flannel.

'Oi!' yelled George, half delighted, half terrified. 'Get off!'

It was a dog. A huge, black shaggy dog with hair on its forehead so long and curly, its eyes were almost invisible. It bowed down in front of George, tail wagging, flashing its giant teeth and enormous pink tongue.

George pushed himself up from the floor. The dog seemed to take this as a cue for a play-fight, whirling around in circles to show how fast he could pounce and strike. It was funny and scary and impressive all at the same time; a show of strength and power without ever being properly threatening.

Where had it come from? Lady Jane and Koko

weren't due back at Hill House until tomorrow, and there were no fishermen at the lake this weekend. The only people on the entire estate were him and his dad . . .

'Midnight! Where are you?'

A man's voice rang out in the darkness.

The dog pricked up its ears, let out a rumbling bark, and bounded off!

Someone was up at Hill House!

CHAPTER THREE

W ho could it be, this late at night?
Burglars?

George needed to find out.
That was one of the things he and his dad were
here for: to look after everything until Lady Jane
and Koko got back from their trip around the
world. George was so jealous of Koko – being
home-schooled on a cruise ship was way more
exciting than reading at his poky kitchen table.

He picked his way through the brambles, heading back to the path, then jogged up through the trees to where it met the gravel drive.

A strange man was standing beside the fountain! He was bathed in moonlight, and wearing an open white-collared shirt, a shiny dark burgundy waistcoat, and a wide-brimmed leather hat.

As George watched, the dog ran up to greet him.

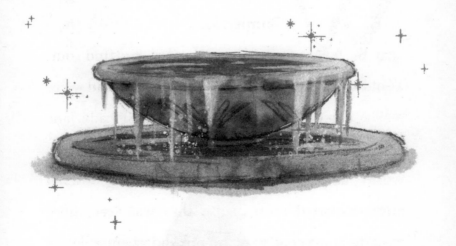

'Midnight! There you are! Where did you run off to?' The man's voice was high and had a London accent.

George gulped: he needed to tell his dad. He was about to run back to the cottage when the lights came on in the hall, and two familiar figures appeared in the doorway: a mother with wavy blonde hair and a daughter with a chestnut ponytail. It was Lady Jane and Koko!

They must have come back early!

'Hi!' shouted George, so delighted to see them that he forgot how late it was, and that no one could see him in the dark.

The dog called Midnight began to bark.

'Who goes there?' called the man.

'It's me!' announced George, stepping into the light. 'George!'

Lady Jane recognized him immediately. 'You've

grown so tall! Koko, look, it's George!'

'Hi, George,' said Koko, grinning. 'It's great to see you!'

'Come here right now,' said Lady Jane. 'And give me a big hug!'

George rushed over, beaming, and wrapped his arms tight around Lady Jane.

'George's father is the estate manager,' explained Lady Jane, turning to the man with the leather hat. 'He and Koko are like brother and sister. George, meet Clive, my new husband.'

'Very pleased to meet you, George,' said Clive, with a little bow.

'Husband?' George was confused. The last he knew, Lady Jane was divorced. Wasn't that why she had gone on the cruise – because she'd split up with Koko's dad and she and Koko needed cheering up?

'Yes, husband.' Clive grinned, checking his watch. 'As of approximately fourteen days, seven hours, and thirty-six minutes ago. Not that I'm counting every wonderful second.'

Clive kissed Lady Jane's hand, and she blushed. George looked at Koko; she was smiling politely, but something in her eyes seemed unsure.

'I hope Midnight didn't wake you with all that howling,' said Clive to George.

The dog's ears pricked at the sound of its name, and it came trotting over.

'Of course not,' said George, to be polite. 'What breed is he?'

'A Pony-Poo. Giant poodle crossed with Shetland pony.'

George laughed politely.

'I'm joking of course,' said Clive. 'No idea, to be honest. Had him since he was a puppy. Some Irish wolfhound in there somewhere, I think. Maybe a pinch of Labrador.'

'He looks like a teddy bear.'

'Tickle him behind his ears,' urged Clive. 'He likes that.'

Midnight let George tickle him, then shook his head free of George's hand, trotted over to the fountain, and began to drink with enormous, human-sounding slurps.

'Can he understand what we're saying?'

'I doubt it,' snorted Clive. 'Just about capable of standing upright, if you ask me.'

'George, I'm sorry we disturbed you this late,' said Lady Jane, opening the boot of the car. 'We were going to come back tomorrow, but Clive just couldn't wait.'

'Midsummer's Night!' exclaimed Clive, rushing to help with the suitcases. 'I said, "Jane, we have

to arrive on Midsummer's Night. It's auspicious."
Do you know what auspicious means, George?'

George shook his head.

'It means *lucky*,' said Clive, dragging a large case
on to the drive. 'From Midsummer's Night to full
moon is a magical time. Now, tell me. Are you
wearing a watch?'

George shook his head.

'Not to worry – here's one I prepared earlier!'
said Clive, snapping his watch from his wrist with
a flourish and offering it to George for inspection.

'You're going to love Clive's tricks,' Lady Jane
said, beaming. 'They're so clever.'

'Now, sir,' said Clive, as if he was performing
onstage. 'Would you be so kind as to place the
watch in this bag?'

Clive produced a purple velvet bag from
his trouser pocket and held it open invitingly.

George looked at Lady Jane.

'Clive's a magician,' she said proudly. 'That's how we met: he was working on the cruise ship.'

'Now, now,' said Clive to Lady Jane. 'Don't give away all my secrets.' He shook the bag, encouraging George to play along. George didn't want to hurt Clive's feelings, so he placed the watch inside.

'Thank you,' said Clive, brandishing a velvet-handled hammer. 'Now WATCH carefully. Pun intended.'

Before George could stop him, Clive placed the bag on the stone base of the fountain and smashed it three times with the hammer!

George's mouth fell open in surprise.

'Then we say the magic words, *Tempus Fugit*!'

Clive gave the bag a little shake.

'Now please,' said Clive smugly. 'Remove the timepiece.'

George did as he was asked, but all he could feel was broken watch parts. He pulled something out: one half of the brown leather strap.

There was a pause.

'That's very strange,' said Clive thoughtfully, peering into the bag. 'Very strange indeed . . .'

'Is there a problem?' asked Lady Jane.

'No,' said Clive, shaking his head. 'No problem. Err . . . There's just going to be an interval, that's all. In the trick. Let's get the stuff in, and I'll do the second part later. Maybe tomorrow, actually, as it's getting a little late.'

'It's gone wrong again,' said Koko, sighing.

'Round of applause for George!' declared Clive quickly.

Lady Jane applauded awkwardly.

George frowned. Could this peculiar man really be Lady Jane's new husband? What was kind, down-to-earth Lady Jane doing with a slimy magician like Clive?

'Come on then!' called Clive hurriedly. 'These bags aren't going to carry themselves!'

CHAPTER FOUR

Gogmagog the giant carp lurched awake, his barbels twitching.

Something was up.

He'd spent the afternoon hoovering up larvae from the mud at the very deepest part of the lake, and for the last hour or so had been resting in the clear water under the willow tree, watching absent-mindedly as the moon climbed higher and higher in the starlit sky.

He rippled his dorsal fin, and began to paddle, flushing tiny currents over his body. The water had a strange taste. It was a taste he recognized — one that spelled danger. But where was it coming from?

With a beat of his tail, Gogmagog powered forward and patrolled the lake. He shimmied through the bulrushes, dived under the fallen tree trunk, then surfaced by the inlet of the stream, flushing its oxygen-rich water over his gills.

This was the source of the scent, no question,

and it was *definitely* familiar. He hovered there, pushing against the incoming current, letting the water soak against him, and suddenly, he knew the answer. A dog was drinking from the fountain.

Dogs meant fishermen. And fishermen meant . . .

Gogmagog shuddered. It was best not to think about it.

He pulsed his tail and retreated to the safest place in the lake: the silky black mud, deep below the branches of the fallen tree.

CHAPTER FIVE

'A dog called Midnight?'

George was back at the cottage, having sprinted home to tell his father about the return of Lady Jane and Koko.

'He belongs to Clive. Lady Jane's new husband.'

'Ah yes,' said Gabe, brushing the crumbs from his lap. 'She mentioned him on the phone. I was pretty surprised about that, to tell you the truth. I hope she knows what she's doing, marrying someone she's only just met. What's he like?'

'He's a magician.'

'A magician?' Gabe raised his eyebrows. 'Lady Jane has married a magician?'

George nodded. 'There's something strange about him, if you ask me.'

'Now, George,' said his father sternly. 'Let's not be mean.'

'Why don't you come and say hello? They've got loads of suitcases and stuff. You could help them unpack?'

Gabe scratched the stubble on his chin, as if he was thinking it over. Then he pushed himself up out of his armchair, drew the curtain back from the window and peered up towards the house.

He stood there for a few seconds, then turned, a happy smile playing on his lips.

'Good to have them back, eh?'

'You've missed her, haven't you?' asked George. 'Lady Jane, I mean.'

Gabe's smile vanished, as if he was worried he had given too much away.

'There's a lot that needs sorting,' he said gruffly, clearing his throat. 'The roof needs fixing, for a start. The lake's going to need dredging at some point and that fountain's been making some strange gurgling noises. Bit of focus from the lady of the house wouldn't go amiss. And I know you'll be glad to have Koko back to keep you company.'

'Go and talk to her,' urged George. 'She's right there!'

Gabe hesitated for a brief moment, glancing back out of the window.

'It's really late, George. We'll go tomorrow,' he said firmly. 'Once they've had a chance to settle in. Besides, you've got school in the morning.'

'I could take the day off?' suggested George. 'That's the great thing about home-schooling, Dad. We call the shots.'

His dad smiled. '*I* call the shots, son. And I'm telling you to go to bed.'

No sooner was George tucked up under the covers, than he heard a strange scratching sound at the window.

He slid out of bed, tiptoed across the rug, pulled back the curtain and jumped!

Midnight was outside, standing with his paws on the sill, his human-like eyes staring directly into George's.

'Midnight!' he exclaimed. 'You scared me!'

A giant paw scratched at the glass.

'Stop it!' scolded George. 'You'll break it!'

The paw swiped again. Gingerly opening the window, George placed a hand on Midnight's curly-haired chest and gave him a gentle push.

'Down, boy,' he whispered. 'Get down!'

Midnight dropped from the sill and turned in a circle. Then he sat upright, panting, clearly wanting something.

'What's the matter? Are you lost?'

Midnight began to whine.

'All right, all right,' whispered George. 'I'll take you home. Then I'm coming straight back, okay? Otherwise I'll get into trouble.'

As quickly and quietly as he could, George struggled back into his dressing gown, shuffled into his slippers, and climbed out of the window into the moonlight.

'Come on,' he whispered to Midnight. 'This way.'

There's something very special about being followed by a dog, and George felt a surge of joy as he and Midnight trotted through the woods towards the gravel drive of the house. For a moment he let himself imagine that Midnight was his very own dog, and that the two of them were going on a Brand-New Adventure. The crunching gravel reminded him of a beach he had once been to, where there were stones instead of sand. Suddenly he and Midnight were a famous pirate and his trusty hunting dog, returning to their ship after an extremely successful night of pirating.

He was about to herd his imaginary flock of stolen sheep across the lawn and up the gangplank, when a door opened in the ship, and it became Hill House again. George froze.

GONG! GONG! GONG!

Clive's silhouette appeared in the doorway, just as the grandfather clock in the hall began to strike midnight. Clive seemed to be acting very suspiciously; looking around him as if he wanted to make sure he wasn't being watched. Even more curiously, he was carrying two animals in cages.

George felt his breathing quicken as Clive, sensing he wasn't alone, peered out into the darkness.

'Who's there?' he whispered sharply.

Before George could stop him, Midnight bounded across the grass, jumped the hedge, and went crashing across the gravel to the bottom of the steps, wagging his tail madly.

'Oh,' said Clive in a half-whisper. 'It's you. *Sssh*. No barking, please. I'm about to conduct a very important experiment.'

Sensing that he shouldn't be seen, George scurried across the lawn and ducked behind the hedge.

Sure that he was alone, Clive tiptoed down the steps of Hill House and made his way towards the fountain. He lifted one of the cages into the moonlight and George could see it contained a yellow-and-green budgerigar. As George watched, the bird tapped a miniature bell with its beak, and a tiny jingle rang out into the night. Next, Clive lifted the second cage, which held a white rabbit.

It wasn't doing very much at all except chewing a very orange carrot.

What was going on?

As if preparing for one of his magic tricks, Clive placed the cages either side of him on the edge of the fountain. Then he reached forward and swirled the water in the basin, round and round, so that it made a whirlpool. He looked up at the moon and closed his eyes.

'Gogmagog, Gogmagog, Gogmagog, Gogmagog!' he chanted.

Opening the budgie's cage, he dipped a finger in the water and fed it a drop. Then he did the same with the rabbit.

Perhaps it was the angle George was watching from, but the surface of the fountain suddenly flashed bright with moonlight, and he had to close his eyes. When he opened them, he saw that both the rabbit and the budgie were puffed up and shaking!

Suddenly, the bunny closed its eyes and flopped on to the floor of its cage. Barely seconds later, the budgie tumbled off its perch and landed flat on its back in a puff of sawdust.

George was horrified. Had Clive killed them both?

The budgie woke first. Its feet began to twitch,

then with a flick of its wings, it rolled over and stood up. It seemed confused; turning its head back and forth to examine its tail, body and wings.

The rabbit woke next, also clearly startled. It craned around to stare at its fluffy tail and pawed its ears as if not used to having them.

'Look, Midnight!' whispered Clive excitedly. 'It worked! I *knew* it was possible – they've swapped bodies!'

Midnight sat upright and panted.

'The budgie is now in the rabbit's body, and the rabbit is in the budgie's.'

As he spoke, he brought out the bird, perched on his finger.

'Watch this.'

Clive plucked the half-eaten carrot from the rabbit's cage, and offered it to the budgie, who pecked at it eagerly.

'You see, Midnight? I knew I was on to a good thing here – the fountain's magic! It's going to make me rich!'

Midnight, picking up on his master's excitement, began to bark!

'*Sssh!*' hissed Clive. '*Sssh!*'

Midnight did as he was told.

'It's a secret, okay? Good dog. Now please excuse me,' said Clive to Midnight, hooking a hands-free earpiece into his ear. 'I have an important call to make.'

Midnight sniffed at the caged rabbit.

'Clarence? It's Clive. I'm at the house.'

Clive took another look around to make sure no one was listening.

'I've got a present for you. One of the jewels I stole, if you want to come and collect it. And when you do . . . let's just say I've got an even tastier proposition for you.'

34

As he spoke, he fed the budgie another morsel of carrot.

'A very tasty proposition indeed.' He chuckled gleefully.

George gasped out loud.

'Who's there?' Clive's head whipped around, searching in the darkness as George ducked back down behind the hedge, his heart racing. Clive had heard him!

'Midnight!' rasped Clive, pointing to exactly where George was hiding. 'Find it!'

George could only watch as Midnight came bounding across the gravel, jumped the low hedge, and gave his cheek an enormous wet lick.

'Is anyone there?' called Clive.

'Good boy,' whispered George in Midnight's ear, praying the dog wouldn't give him away. 'Good boy.'

Clive was standing on tiptoe, staring right at them. He seemed to be deciding whether or not to come over and join the search. George shut his eyes tight, desperate not to get caught!

'Come on then,' called Clive.

Midnight gave George one more friendly lick, then jumped the hedge and went bouncing back across the gravel, throwing himself at Clive's feet.

'Good lad,' said Clive, petting Midnight's head. 'I know you'd tell me if we had an intruder.' He put the budgie back, picked up the two cages, and headed back towards the house.

George breathed a sigh of relief then immediately frowned. Had he *really* just seen a budgie swap bodies with a rabbit? And what was all this about stealing jewels? Was Clive some sort of thief?

Who was the real Clive, and what was he up to?

CHAPTER SIX

At breakfast the following morning, Gabe handed George the old book from the night before.

'What's this?' mumbled George through a mouthful of hot buttered toast. His mind was racing, replaying what he'd seen at the fountain last night.

'Your task for the week,' replied his dad. 'You know what yesterday was?'

'Yes,' said George confidently. 'It was Sunday.'

'Yes, it was Sunday,' said Gabe, taking his plate to the sink. 'But it was also something else.'

'The night Lady Jane and Koko came home?'

'It was Midsummer's Night. So I thought you could read that.'

His father was busy scraping his plate into the bin, so George took the opportunity to wipe his buttery hands on the tablecloth. He examined the spine of the book.

'*A Midsummer Night's Dream.*'

'That's right,' said Gabe, scrubbing the plate  under the tap. 'By an up-and-coming writer called William Shakespeare.'

'Shakespeare?' George groaned. 'Isn't that a bit boring?'

'I don't know,' said Gabe, placing the sparkling-clean plate carefully in the draining rack. 'Do you find magic boring? Is a man swapping heads with a donkey boring?'

'S-sorry?' choked George, wondering if his dad could read his mind and somehow knew that Clive had magically body-swapped a rabbit and a budgie. For a moment, he considered telling Gabe what he had seen the previous night. Then he remembered how cross his father had been when George had said Clive was weird, and thought better of it.

'Right,' said Gabe, not hearing him as he headed for the door. 'I'm going to call in on Lady Jane.'

'Can I come?'

Gabe pointed at the book. 'You've got work to do.' And with that, he closed the door to the cottage firmly behind him, and marched off in the direction of Hill House.

George chewed the inside of his cheek thoughtfully. Obviously there was *A Midsummer Night's Dream* to read . . . But then there was the real-life magic he had witnessed at the fountain. Magic that he needed to tell Koko about.

Cautiously, he edged around the cottage to the far window, watching as Gabe headed off through the woods. As soon as his dad was out of sight, George chucked his plate in the sink and ran after him.

By the time George caught him up, Gabe was striding up the gravel drive towards Hill House. Luckily it was lined with large rhododendron

bushes, so George was able to scoot between them without being seen. It had been hot and dry for days, and little puffs of dust kicked up every time Gabe took a step. The front door was open, but Gabe ignored it, following the path that led to the back of the house. There was no choice now but to walk on the gravel, so George waited until his dad had rounded the corner, then scurried after him.

George watched from around the corner of the house as Gabe approached the back door. There was a loud bark from inside, and the door opened to reveal Clive, wearing an orange silk dressing gown, with Midnight on a leash, pink tongue hanging out and wagging his tail.

'Leave it!' shouted Clive to Midnight, as if the dog was about to attack, which it most definitely wasn't. 'I said leave it!'

Gabe waited patiently as Clive tried various

methods to calm a dog that didn't need calming.

'Careful,' warned Clive, in a tone that made George wonder whether he was trying to scare Gabe. 'Once he sees that we're friends, he'll calm down. Look, Midnight, *friend*. See? We're shaking hands.'

Gabe forced a smile and shook Clive's hand. Midnight, of course, just carried on panting and flicking his bushy tail.

'Mortified,' said Clive, with fake embarrassment. 'Absolutely mortified. He's just so . . . *vicious*. To strangers, that is. Not to family, of course. How can I help you?'

'I've come to introduce myself, sir. I'm the estate manager, Gabriel Oates.'

'The estate manager! Yes, of course. Lady Jane has mentioned you. Clive Blaise. Stage name, of course. Real name is Tooth, Clive Tooth. Doesn't look as good on the posters! Very pleased to meet you. Jane said you run the lake?'

'Amongst other things.'

'How's it going? Gogmagog still very much in evidence, I hear?'

'Still not been caught, but he's in there all right. Saw him myself the day before yesterday. He gets very bold in the off season. He knows we're closed, you see.'

'Closed?'

'That's right. There's no fishing from March till the first full moon after Midsummer.'

'How wonderfully old-fashioned,' said Clive, counting on his fingers. 'So one, two . . . three more nights to go. And after that . . . ? I'd love to try my hand.'

'Ah. I'm afraid we're booked up with paying customers until—'

But Clive cut him off.

'I fished it once, many years ago with my father. That's how Jane and I got talking on the cruise ship. "Where are you from?" I asked her. This was after my magic show, of course. Which she *loved* . . . I mean, our passenger approval ratings were through the roof . . . Sorry, where was I?'

'You asked Lady Jane where she was from.' Gabe forced another smile.

George couldn't help wondering whether a man like Clive, who said such a lot, was ever going to get along with a man like his dad, who said so little.

'Yes of course. "Where are you from?" I asked. "Herefordshire," she said. "Best carp fishing I've ever had was in Herefordshire, at a lake called Greenmire," I said. "That's our lake!" she said. "No?" I said. "Yes! What a coincidence," she said. "There's a fish in there the size of a suitcase," I said. "Huge

45

great thing. They call him—" "Gogmagog!" she said. "After the last giant in England!" . . . And that was it. We've been—'

'Finishing each other's sentences ever since,' said Lady Jane, arriving at the back door.

Gabe's face lit up.

George had been right; it was clear that his dad had missed Lady Jane.

'It's good to have you back, Lady Jane.'

'You know me better than that, Gabe. It's just Jane. I see you've met my *husband*.'

'I still can't get used to that!' Clive beamed, planting a kiss on Lady Jane's cheek that looked even wetter than one of Midnight's licks.

'Congratulations,' said Gabe.

'We got hitched in New York,' explained Clive. 'On the homeward leg. Spur-of-the-moment stuff. I said to her, "I never managed to hook Gogmagog—"'

'But I still landed the big fish!' finished Lady Jane.

Clive and Jane collapsed into giggles. Gabe gave a pained smile and stared at his work boots.

'Speaking of which . . .' tried Clive. 'Gabe was just telling me the lake's closed for fishing.' Clive raised his eyebrows at Lady Jane as if to say: *Do something.*

'We've a few more days before the season starts,' Gabe said firmly.

'Don't look at me, Clive,' said Lady Jane. 'Gabriel's in charge. Now come on,' she said, taking Gabe by the arm. 'I want to hear all about how you and George have been getting on.'

George watched as the three adults went inside. Clive's suspicious behaviour the night before meant he was definitely up to something, and now his dad was obviously on edge. Maybe Clive was the sort of magician you found in books – an evil one who could do *real* magic. George needed to find Koko.

Taking care not to attract anyone's attention, George crept away from his hiding place and scurried back round to the open front door, poking his head into the hall.

The house smelled damp and sad, like it had been crying while everyone was away. George needed to be quick — Gabe might head home at any moment — so he threaded his way through the maze of antique furniture in the sitting room and into the warm brick and bright glass of the orangery.

Koko was sitting just where he expected her to be: on her father's stool, with her back to the door, staring at the empty easel that haunted the middle of the room. This was where Koko's father, Mr Yoshida, had done all his painting; until the divorce, when he had left and gone back to Japan. Back then, this room had been full of crazy colour; Mr Yoshida loved waves, and painted them in every size, colour and shape you could imagine. But now he had gone, and the paintings had washed away with him.

'You okay?' asked George.

Koko didn't move.

'So what was it like? The cruise?'

'We saw my dad in Osaka,' she replied. 'And we visited some cool places. But the bits in between were really boring. There was no one to talk to on the ship. Just lots of old people.' She turned and smiled. 'And I missed you and Gabe.'

George grinned and nodded. 'We missed you too.'

At the sound of a door being pushed open, George turned to see Midnight padding towards him. He stretched out his hand, and the dog gave it a friendly lick.

'Midnight's great though – you're so lucky to have a dog like him.' George paused, unsure how Koko might react. 'What do you think of Clive?' he asked carefully. 'Do you like him?'

'I guess,' Koko replied. 'Why?'

'This is going to sound weird.'

She spun round to face him.

'Tell me.'

George took a deep breath. 'I saw something really strange last night.'

'What sort of something?'

'After you went to bed, Midnight came and got me. I followed him back to the house and saw Clive outside . . .'

George bit his lip anxiously.

'What?'

'He did something, Koko. By the fountain. He had a bunny rabbit—'

'A bunny rabbit?'

'And a bird in a cage. And . . . I think he cast some sort of spell.'

'What sort of spell?'

'A body-swap spell.'

Koko rolled her eyes.

'That can't be true.'

'I swear! The rabbit went into the bird's body, and the bird went into the rabbit's body.'

'How could you possibly know if they'd swapped? They didn't tell you. It must have been a trick – Clive *is* a magician you know. Although that trick he did with the watch didn't exactly work.'

'I saw it, Koko! With my own eyes!' insisted George. 'He was talking to Midnight as he was doing it! Then after the swap, he called some guy called Clarence on his phone.'

There was a flicker of recognition in Koko's eyes.

'Do you know him?' pressed George.

Koko nodded. 'He's Clive's assistant. In his magic act.'

'Clive told Clarence he had a present for him. One of the jewels.'

'*Jewels?* He said that exact word?'

'I swear,' said George. 'What do you think he meant?'

Koko looked closely at George, as if she was deciding whether or not to trust him. Taking a deep breath, she leaned in closer and spoke in a whisper.

'Something strange happened on the ship. A lady accused Clive of stealing her necklace when he was doing a trick during the show. She said Clive swapped it for a fake one.'

'Did he?'

Koko shrugged, but she looked worried.

'Clive said she wasn't remembering it right. She was quite old, and everyone believed him.'

'Koko, if *jewels* means *the necklace*, then Clive must be a criminal!'

They stared at each other, shocked at the news, until Midnight suddenly barked and ran to the door. Lady Jane's voice rang out from the sitting room.

'Koko. Time to go! Oh, hello, George,' said Lady Jane, arriving in the doorway. 'Sorry to drag her away, but she's got a hair appointment, then the optician and the dentist. All the things we've been putting off for the last six months. And I want to go and choose Clive a welcome-home present too. Come on, love.'

Lady Jane beamed happily, clearly expecting Koko to follow.

'Come back after supper,' Koko whispered to George as she got up to leave. 'And we'll investigate.'

CHAPTER SEVEN

B ack at the cottage, the day seemed to drag on for ever. For the rest of the morning, George sat at the kitchen table, trying to focus on *A Midsummer Night's Dream* and failing miserably.

All the names in the story were odd – things like *Hippolyta* and *Theseus* – and the language was so old-fashioned – *our nuptial hour draws on apace* – that before long he found himself hoping that if he lay with his head on the book, the story might magically jump into his brain . . .

The next thing he knew, the front door rattled, and George woke up with a start to find his dad returning home for lunch.

'Where are you up to?' asked Gabe, taking off his work boots.

'The dream,' bluffed George, doing his best to look enthusiastic. 'And I'm really into it.'

His father smiled.

'George, there is no dream. That's sort of the point. Weird and wonderful things happen, but they are all true. At the end Oberon, the king of the fairies, casts a spell so that everyone *thinks* it was a dream. And the characters in the story are happy to believe him.'

'Exactly,' said George. 'That's what I meant.'

'So come on, whereabouts are you in the story?'

George pulled a face. 'Kind of nowhere.'

'Nowhere?' His father was doing his very best to look kind and patient, but George could see disappointment in his eyes.

'Sorry, Dad. I just feel really tired.'

'It's okay,' said his father. 'It's my fault, I guess. I shouldn't have let you stay up so late.'

There wasn't much to say after that. His dad made them both cheese sandwiches, which really weren't George's favourite, but George knew better than to complain when Gabe was already upset with him for not doing his reading.

I'll make it up to him, thought George to himself. *This afternoon I'll work extra hard.*

But as soon as his dad had gone, and he opened the book, once again he found himself drifting off to sleep.

When he woke, the sun was low in the trees, and there was a note by his elbow, held in place by his dad's favourite coffee cup. It read:

George,
Gone to my game. Back at 9.30 p.m. Any probs, ask Lady Jane.
Dinner in fridge. Three minutes in microwave.
Love, Dad
P.S. You need an early night.

Of *course* – Monday nights were his dad's Squash Night, when he played with his friend Spike at the sports centre.

The fact that Gabe was out that evening was very good news indeed; it meant the coast was clear for George to go and find Koko. After all, they had some important investigating to do.

As soon as he'd pinged the pasta and tomato sauce in the microwave, and sloshed it down with a glass of orange juice, George jogged through the woods and up the gravel drive to the front door of Hill House.

He was about to press the bell when Koko, who had clearly been waiting for him, snatched open the door. She poked her head out to check no one was watching, then she closed the door swiftly behind her and put her finger to her lips. She was holding a notebook and pencil and clearly in Detective Mode.

'Operation Fountain is go,' she said with her best serious face. 'Please state our objective.'

'Right,' said George, thrilled to have his playmate back. 'First, we need to find out if Clive really did magic last night.'

'Agreed,' replied Koko, scribbling in her notebook. 'And how do we do that?'

'Easy. We check the rabbit and the budgie and see if they've swapped bodies.'

'Got it,' said Koko. 'So where are they?'

'No idea.' George shrugged. 'Let's ask Clive.'

'But . . . what if he won't tell us?'

'Then we'll know he's up to something!' George smiled.

They found Clive and Lady Jane relaxing in the drawing room; a room as clutter-free and relaxed as the sitting room was crowded and cramped. Gabe had once said that the sitting room was the face Lady Jane thought she should show to the world, full of the trappings of her ancestors, while the drawing room was who she really was: simple and cosy. Clive was wearing shorts, sandals, and his leather hat, and reading a large magazine called *Magician's Monthly*; Lady Jane was sat at her desk in a long floaty dress, making one of her shell necklaces.

Midnight was sprawled in front of the fireplace, doing a very good impression of a large black sheepskin rug. He looked up as George and Koko entered, his ears cocked. He gave the air a couple of experimental sniffs, just to make sure it was them, then lay back down again.

'Clive?' asked Koko.

'Hmm?' replied Clive, without looking up.

'Can we play with the bunny rabbit?'

The magazine came down abruptly. Clive shot a quick glance at Lady Jane, who was busy threading a particularly fiddly piece of shell.

'He's not really a pet, Koko,' he said with a smile. 'He's a working animal.'

'What about the budgie?'

'Sorry, Koko,' said Clive, sipping the dregs of a glass of red wine. 'No can do. Why don't you play with Midnight? He'd love that.'

Midnight sat up. He looked from Clive to the two children as if to say: *Did someone want me?*

'Can we at least look at them?'

'Koko?'

Lady Jane had put down her crafting, and was staring over the top of an imposing pair of half-moon reading glasses. 'You heard what Clive said.'

'They're best left alone, Koko,' added Clive apologetically.

As soon as they were out of the room, the two detectives compared notes.

'He's acting guilty, don't you think?' whispered George.

'I guess,' replied Koko thoughtfully.

George felt something wet on his hand and looked down to see Midnight panting up at him. He was feeling more confident with the dog now, and gave him a little scratch behind his ears. This time Midnight seemed to like it.

'Where do you think he keeps them? The rabbit and the budgie, I mean.'

'The garage,' replied Koko with certainty.

But she was wrong. All that was in there was a broken old pram and Lady Jane's fishing tackle.

'Anywhere else they could be?' asked George as they wandered back into the house.

They were now in the boot room, and Midnight took the opportunity to drink some water from his bowl. He was a very thirsty dog, but George couldn't blame him; it was warm, and he was wearing an enormous fur coat.

Koko looked thoughtful. 'I can't think. The garage is the only obvious place, really. They aren't in their bedroom, or anywhere in the house that I've seen.'

'What's he like? Clive?'

Koko shrugged. 'He makes Mum happy, and she's been really sad since she and Dad split up, so that's good. And he was kind to us on the cruise. But . . .'

'But what?'

'It's been so quick. Seems like one day they met; the next day they married. So I only know what he's like on the outside. And I miss Dad – I don't know why he had to move all the way back to Japan. I only saw him for a couple of days on the cruise—'

Which was when they heard Clive's voice in the hallway.

'Look what I've just found in the wine cellar! Chateau Beaumains 1945! This place just keeps on giving!'

Clive's footsteps crossed the hall and the sitting room door closed with a loud *thunk*.

Koko looked at George.

'Of course!' she hissed. 'They must be in the catacomb!'

CHAPTER EIGHT

'Right, there are the matches. Where's the torch?'

Koko was in the kitchen, searching through the drawers. The catacomb was a huge cellar, underneath the house. It was the perfect place to hide something, because it was always pitch dark. It was also George's least favourite place in the entire world.

'Is that it?' asked George, reluctantly, pointing

to where the torch was sitting on one of the shelves. He had spotted it as soon as they'd entered, and half wished he hadn't.

Koko pulled a chair out from under the kitchen table, stood on it, and grabbed the torch. She flicked the switch a few times to make sure it was working, then leaped off the chair, ready for action.

'Come on.' Her eyes were bright with excitement. 'Let's check it out.'

Koko hurriedly led George to the hallway, then to a door behind the main staircase. Midnight, who didn't seem to understand the secret mission they were on, trotted contentedly alongside them, snuffling noisily.

The door to the catacomb was made to look like part of the hallway wall; the only thing that gave it away was the handle. Koko opened it to reveal a rickety narrow staircase, plunging down into darkness.

'Stay close,' whispered Koko, switching on the torch. 'So you don't lose your footing.'

'Can we be quick? You know I don't like coming down here,' said George anxiously.

'Don't be such a wimp.'

'Come on, Koko. It's really creepy.'

'Creepy how?'

'There are graves in there.'

'Tombs,' corrected Koko. 'I think they're beautiful.' She grinned. 'Come on,' she beckoned. 'Midnight hates stairs, so he can stand guard.'

George was having second, third and fourth thoughts, but it was too late: Koko was already edging her way down the rickety staircase.

George took a deep breath, gave Midnight a reassuring pat, then followed Koko down the narrow stairs, with one hand against the wall for balance. The stairway turned, the wall became a banister, and a second flight of open steps led downwards. They were up high, in the middle of the catacomb, and a row of ancient stone archways stretched out on either side of them.

'Ghost!' gasped Koko, flashing the torch beam from a stack of cobwebbed wine bottles on to three large shadowy stone boxes.

'Aaagh!' George's heart leaped right into his mouth, and Koko had to steady him before he went tumbling down the stairs.

'Koko!' He scowled. 'Stop it!'

Koko dissolved into giggles.

'It's not funny!' huffed George. He nodded towards the nearest tombs. 'Whose are they?' he asked shakily.

'I dunno.' Koko shrugged. 'Distant relatives of

mine, I guess. They don't bury people here any more – these are all really old. Mum says one of them's a crusader.'

They were now at the bottom of the stairs.

'This way,' whispered Koko, turning away from the tombs and wine bottles, into the other half of the room.

'Does it make you feel weird?' whispered George. 'Living in a house with graves underneath it?'

'No,' said Koko, shining the torch around the first alcove, which was full of junk. 'It's comforting. Like they're looking after us.'

George thought about that for a moment.

'My mum gave me a puppy once,' he said. 'To look after me. But my dad gave it away.'

Koko held the torch so they could see each other's eyes. George was surprised at himself. He'd never told anyone about Snowball before. Perhaps it was the dream he'd had last night that made him say it.

'When was this?'

'Before we moved here.'

'I don't understand,' said Koko gently. 'If the dog was supposed to look after you, why did your dad give it away?'

'I'm not sure exactly. When Mum died . . . Dad acted a bit strangely for a while. I think it was a bit much to manage everything, but he's better now.'

'What was its name?'

George smiled. Koko loved animals just as much as he did.

'Snowball. She was an albino.'

'Wow. That's rare, right?'

'Really rare. An albino chihuahua.'

'And where is she now?'

George shrugged. 'I don't know. Mum got her from a dog rescue, so I guess Dad took her back there. I just hope Snowball's not . . . you know . . . sad about it. Being part of our family for a little bit then having to go back, I mean.'

'If she was a puppy,' said Koko, putting a hand on George's shoulder, 'she wouldn't remember. So don't worry.'

'You're right.' George nodded. 'Thanks.'

'I'm sure she found another home.'

Something moved on the ceiling, and Koko responded with the torch.

'Bats,' she said.

Hanging upside down were a dozen or so sleeping bats, each of them no bigger than a fist, their furry heads just visible between tightly wrapped leathery wings.

'And look!' whispered Koko, swishing the beam to where a crimson-and-gold cloth was poking out from one of the furthest arches.

They edged closer. The cloth was draped over a wooden table and sitting proudly on top of it was a large old-fashioned book open on a gold stand, a gold candelabra with three candles, and what looked to George very much like the rabbit and budgie cages, each draped in purple silk cloth.

'Here,' said Koko, handing George the torch. She struck a match and lit one of the candles. The flame reached the wax and began to shine brightly, pushing back the inky darkness. Koko lifted one cloth, while George pulled back the other, to reveal the rabbit and the budgerigar. The rabbit was nibbling at a piece of carrot, and the budgie was pecking at a feeder full of sunflower seeds.

'Hmm,' mused Koko. 'They look pretty normal to me.'

George revealed the rabbit and the budgerigar

'Maybe Clive switched them back,' offered George.

'It's possible,' said Koko doubtfully.

'Or they've just got used to it.'

Koko frowned. 'What do you mean?'

'Well, think about it. If you and I swapped bodies, to start off with we'd be really freaked out. I'd want to eat the things I usually eat, and do the things I usually do. Then after a while, I'd get used to it. Being in each other's bodies, I mean.'

'Hmm,' said Koko again, in a way that made George sure she still didn't believe him about the whole Clive-casting-a-spell thing.

Maybe the book would prove it.

George started to read. It wasn't easy, because the words looked very old-fashioned.

'What does it say?' asked Koko.

'The Fong of Gogmagog.'

'*Song*,' corrected Koko. '"The Song of Gogmagog."

In olden times they used to print *S*s like *F*s. Here.'

Koko cleared her throat and began to read aloud.

On a hilltop stands a fountain
A brimming basin carved in stone
Aged a thousand years and counting
Springing from a source unknown.

On a hilltop stands a fountain
From its basin spills a stream
Down the hillside, through a woodland
Over rocks and into reeds.

There it finds its destination:
A lake that stretches far and wide
With waters sweet and clear as crystal
Its bottom deeper than desire——

'Wait!' said George. 'That sounds just like Hill House! We've got a fountain, a stream, and a lake! What's this book called?'

Koko pulled back the cover. '*The Book of Shadows.*'

George swallowed.

'Koko . . .' he whispered. 'I think this is a book of spells.'

Koko ignored him and kept on reading.

In this lake there lurks a monster
With gaping mouth and eyes agog
Its size beyond imagination
A giant known as Gogmagog!

Gogmagog, he holds a secret:
Past Midsummer, before full moon,
Should a charmer take two creatures
Then stir the water round the moon.

Call his name, three times repeat it
One drop of water each consume:
Their souls shall switch, their bodies cheated
Marching to each other's tune!

'That's it!' said George excitedly. 'That's the spell he must have done last night! I heard him say it!'

'Explain,' demanded Koko.

'It's sort of in code,' said George. 'But I think what it means is: if you have two creatures, then you swirl the water in the fountain, say "Gogmagog" four times – which is what I heard Clive do – then make each creature drink a drop, they'll switch bodies!'

Koko wasn't saying anything, and George could see that she wasn't sure.

'Clive's up to no good, Koko. I know he's in your family now, but he's planning something – I'm sure of it.'

A bright white light flashed at the top of the stairs.

'Hello?'

It was Clive's voice, high and nasal, and the light was coming from his phone.

George and Koko stared at each other, frozen in fear.

'Is anybody there?'

CHAPTER NINE

Quick as a flash, George threw the silk cloths back over the budgie and the rabbit, and Koko blew out the candle. There was the creak of footsteps, and the light on Clive's phone began to dance. He was coming down the stairs!

'Over there!' hissed Koko, clicking off her torch and pulling George behind a pile of packing crates.

George closed his eyes. His heart was racing.

He breathed in deeply, and peeked around the corner of the crate. Clive's sandals appeared on one of the lower steps; then his knee-length lemon-coloured socks; then his red tartan shorts; then finally his tummy, rounded shoulders and leather hat, shadowed by the light on his phone.

'Koko?' he called. 'Are you in there?'

At the top of the stairs, Midnight barked.

'Is that a yes or a no?' asked Clive, looking back up at the dog.

Midnight didn't answer.

'Dogs, honestly,' muttered Clive to himself. 'What are they good for?'

There was more creaking as he descended the last few steps, then a shuffling as he crossed the dusty stone floor.

The light from his phone scanned the walls of the catacomb.

'*Children*,' he crooned. 'Come out wherever you are.'

George held his breath, scared to make even the slightest sound.

The light grew brighter, and the shuffling came nearer, until Clive was right beside them, on the other side of the packing cases!

'Hello, you two.'

He'd seen them! George sighed and hung his head in disappointment. He began to climb out from behind the crate, only to realize that Clive was talking to the budgie and the rabbit! Quick as a flash, he ducked back behind the crate!

'It's time we paid another visit to that fountain,' said Clive in a sing-song voice.

Then off went his sandals, scuffing across the stone floor, taking the white light of his phone with them.

George and Koko waited in silence until the door shut, leaving them in the pitch black.

'We need to follow him!' said George. 'He's going to cast another spell!'

'Back door,' said Koko, clicking on the torch.

Bursting back into the hallway, Koko quickly led George to the boot room, then out through the back door.

Clive was crouched beside the fountain, holding the rabbit and the budgie in their cages. Creeping as close as they dared, George and Koko watched from behind the hedge as he solemnly put his hand in the basin and began to stir the water. This time George noticed he moved it anticlockwise, not clockwise.

Midnight, who was sitting on the grass nearby, yawned and lay down with his head between his paws, as if truly bored.

Clive spread his arms wide and began to chant while staring up at the moon. 'Gogmagog, Gogmagog, Gogmagog, Gogmagog!' Then he dipped his finger in the water and fed the rabbit a drop.

'You see?' whispered George. 'He's putting a drop of water on its tongue.'

Koko looked doubtful.

'Watch,' insisted George. 'He'll do the same with the budgie.'

Sure enough, Clive opened the budgie's cage and performed a similar action. Once again the fountain's surface flashed with moonlight, dazzling the two children so that they had to look away.

'Now they'll both fall over,' whispered George.

Right on cue, the budgie dropped off its perch, and the rabbit flopped over on its side. Koko gave a low whistle.

Clive gave each animal a tiny nudge, but they remained motionless.

After a breathless minute, the budgie flapped its wings, and began to chirrup excitedly. The rabbit pawed its own face, as if waking from a deep sleep; then it too sniffed the air and scratched its ear with its hind leg, happy to be alive.

Delighted, Clive pulled the rabbit out from its cage and offered it a carrot, which it began to nibble happily.

'Who's the Master?' asked Clive to Midnight, who carried on ignoring him. 'Yeah! Who's the Mage? Who's the Main Man?'

Clive's phone rang, and he tucked his handsfree into his ear.

'Clarence! You can make it? Oh, that's fantastic news . . . See you tomorrow. And err . . . that tasty proposition I told you about?'

There was a pause while he fed the rabbit another morsel of carrot.

'Well it just got even tastier.'

Grinning broadly, Clive stowed the rabbit and carried both cages back up the steps to Hill House.

Once they were sure the coast was clear, George and Koko emerged from behind the hedge.

'You see?' said George.

'Not really.' He could tell that Koko wanted to believe him.

'What do you mean, "not really"? You saw it with your own eyes!' George felt his frustration rising. 'Clive reversed the spell!'

'What I saw,' levelled Koko, 'was a man give a rabbit and a budgie a drink of water.'

George sighed.

'It was different the first time,' he admitted. 'They looked so freaked out. That's how I knew they'd swapped bodies.'

'Sorry, George,' said Koko. 'I get that Clive's been acting weird. But this body-swap thing? It's kind of hard to believe. Tell me one more time exactly what you saw, and this time I'll make notes.'

Koko took out her notebook and pen, ready to write everything down.

George paused, trying to find the correct words. 'First, Clive put them both on the edge of the fountain; the rabbit and the budgie. Then he swirled the water like this . . .'

George dipped his hand in the water and the moon's reflection disintegrated into countless swirling stars.

'Then he said: "Gogmagog, Gogmagog, Gogmagog, Gogmagog." Then he dabbed a drop of water on their tongues. Like this . . .'

George was just dabbing a drop of water on his own tongue, when he heard a slurping noise beside him. Midnight had climbed up from his seat on the grass, and now had his head in the fountain, taking a noisy drink.

George's jaw dropped.

'Midnight! Stop! Don't drink the water!' he yelled.

But it had been a long, hot day, and Midnight was very thirsty.

George desperately grabbed the dog by its collar and tried to pull him back!

'George, don't be mean!' protested Koko. 'He's really thirsty!'

There was a blinding flash of moonlight, and George began to feel dizzy.

'George?' asked Koko. 'Are you okay?'

'I've cast the spell by mistake!'

Koko laughed. 'That's crazy.'

'I'm serious, Koko,' muttered George, fighting to stay awake. 'I'm turning into a . . . do-o-o-og!'

And then everything went dark.

CHAPTER TEN

'George? George?'

He could hear Koko's voice, calling him.

George opened his eyes. Everything was blurry, as if he was underwater. The colours he could see looked like they were underwater too: just blues, yellows and greys. He tried to rub his eyes, but instead of a hand, up came a black furry paw!

'*What's going on?*' he tried to say, but all

that came out was a series of barks.

'George? Are you okay?'

He glanced up at Koko. But she wasn't talking to him, she was talking to a boy, slumped on the ground beside them; a boy that looked just like him.

It had really happened – he'd swapped bodies with Midnight!

Koko shook the boy's shoulder.

'George, wake up.'

The boy opened his eyes.

'What happened?' he murmured. 'Wait . . .'

He sat up in alarm, staring at his human body in disbelief.

'I've got hands!'

'George, stop being silly!' scolded Koko.

'I'm not George; I'm Midnight!' exclaimed the boy, holding up his hands, then immediately

It had really happened — he'd swapped bodies with Midnight!

becoming fascinated with them again. 'Oh wow – I've always wanted these! You wouldn't believe how hard it is to open a door with your mouth . . . Wait, I can talk! And look – I'm walking on two feet. I'm as tall as you are!'

'George, time for bed!'

Gabe was calling from further down the drive.

'George,' said Koko to the boy. 'Your dad's calling you.'

'I'm not George,' insisted the boy. 'I'm Midnight!'

'Stop it!' said Koko, half laughing. 'You're freaking me out.'

'Time to come in now, Koko! It's getting late.'

Lady Jane was standing at the door of Hill House.

'George, come on!' called Gabe impatiently.

'Oh hello, Gabe,' called Lady Jane. 'I didn't see

you there. Garden in the morning?'

'Absolutely,' agreed Gabe. 'Soon as I've checked the fences. Now I'd better get this one to bed. He's been burning the candle at both ends and in the middle. Come on, George. Come quietly or I'll have to make a citizen's arrest.'

But the boy didn't move.

'George! You've got to go!' urged Koko, pulling the boy to his feet and pushing him in Gabe's direction.

'Look at me!' exclaimed Midnight. 'Two legs! I am never going to get used to this!'

He lurched down the gravel drive, with George trotting alongside him, desperate to see what would happen.

'Goodnight, George!' called Koko from the top of the steps.

'George is the dog,' called Midnight, pointing straight at George. 'I'm Midnight.'

They reached Gabe, who was now looking extremely puzzled.

'George?' he asked suspiciously. 'Are you okay?'

'Sorry,' said Midnight, sniffing the air. 'I'm pretty sure you're George's dad, but I've lost my sense of smell. Do you mind if I sniff your bum?'

'Excuse me?' asked Gabe, not entirely sure he'd heard correctly.

'Or a lick? Can I give you a lick?'

'No you cannot give me a lick,' said Gabe irritably, taking the cottage path. 'What's got into you?'

'Can you slow down a bit?' asked Midnight as they reached the trees. 'I'm finding this walking thing really tricky.'

'George, I'm serious. What's going on? Have you been drinking?'

'I keep telling you, that's George there. I'm Midnight.'

'*He's right!*' yelled George. But once again, all that came out was an excited bark!

'Off you go, Midnight,' said Gabe, pointing back along the path. 'Go on!'

'*Dad, it's me!*' shouted George, but all that came out was a volley of barks.

'Here!' said Gabe, picking something up from beside the cottage door. 'What's this?'

A stick! George felt a surge of excitement chase down his spine. Something felt good back there, and he craned his neck to see what it was. Of course, his tail was wagging!

'Fetch!' called Gabe, and in slow motion, George saw him draw back his hand and launch the stick into the air. It arced up into the trees, turning and twisting, and George began to run! Nothing was more important than getting that stick.

In slow motion, the stick began to fall, and at

what he knew to be precisely the right moment, George leaped! His jaws clamped shut, snatching the stick out of the sky. He'd caught it!

Landing hard on the ground, his whole body flooded with joy. He began to pant, and as the delicious night air filled his lungs, the world sped back up into real time.

He turned to look for Gabe, tail wagging furiously . . .

Just in time to hear the door of the cottage slam shut.

CHAPTER ELEVEN

George was completely baffled. How could his dad shut him out like that?

A dark thought crossed his mind: maybe Gabe didn't really like dogs. He had only thrown the stick because he wanted to get rid of him. To his father, he was now just Clive's annoying dog Midnight. And Midnight was his beloved son George.

He felt a pang of jealousy. The cottage was his

home, and he was locked out! Somehow, he had to tell his dad what had happened, and reverse the swap.

He closed his eyes and took in a lungful of air. Being a dog was like having superpowers; he just needed to use them to his advantage. His vision might be colourless and blurry, but he realized his nose gave him a perfect picture of everything around him: the cottage, with its musty lichen-covered walls and mossy slate roof; the mouldering cedar-chip path under his feet; and above his head, the sweet-smelling beech trees of the woods.

His hearing was next level too: if he really focused, he could pick up a caterpillar munching on a blade of grass; the birds twittering in the treetops; the rabbits scuffling in the brambles; and the crystal-clear voices of Gabe and Midnight.

'Err . . . I think there's been some sort of mistake,' Midnight was saying.

'What sort of mistake?' asked Gabe.

George sniffed the ground: there was the outline of his father's boot, as clear as if he had left a footprint. And there was another. He tracked them to the door of the cottage, and sniffed the handle, finding the scent of his father's hand. If only he could see inside . . .

'I should be out there,' Midnight was saying.

'Don't be ridiculous, George. It's way past your bedtime.'

Of course! The window. George reared himself up on to his hind legs, and placed his paws on the sill. Luckily the curtains were still open: Midnight was by the door, just out of sight; and Gabe was sitting at the kitchen table, staring at him in exasperation.

'But I'm not George,' Midnight protested.

'I keep saying that, but you won't believe me.'

'Oh really?' asked Gabe, folding his arms. 'Who are you then?'

'Midnight. You know, Clive's dog! The fountain at the front of the house cast some sort of weird spell. George has gone into my body, and I've gone into his.'

Gabe sighed and shook his head.

'George, you're nearly ten. Don't you think you're getting a bit old for these games?'

'But it's true!'

'Okay, fine, you're a dog,' said Gabe wearily. 'It's still bedtime. Now . . . do you want anything to eat?'

There was a pause. Midnight's mouth tried to form words, but failed.

'Sorry . . .' he said eventually. 'Could you ask me that again?'

Gabe shrugged. 'Are you hungry?'

Midnight narrowed his eyes.

'Yes . . . I'm hungry . . . Why?'

'Help yourself to anything you want from the fridge.'

Midnight laughed. 'Nice one,' he said, pointing a finger at Gabe. 'You almost had me there.'

Gabe looked confused.

Midnight's face fell. 'Oh my days! You're actually serious! You really mean it.'

He rushed to the fridge, and threw open the door.

'Of course! I'm a human. I'm your son,' he said, seizing the Key lime pie left over from Sunday lunch. 'Therefore I am allowed to have anything I want from the fridge!'

Midnight took an enormous bite. 'Oh wow,' he said, his mouth crammed with crunchy biscuit and delicious lime cream. 'This is good. I can have anything from the fridge, right? Anything at all.'

George's neck hair suddenly stood on end, and a low growl rumbled its way up from his belly. He was angry! His ears flattened against his head, and his tail stopped twitching, going stiff as a pole. Midnight was in his home, with his dad, eating his food!

'*Stop!*' he yelled. '*Stop that right now!*'

But of course, the angry bark that came out made Gabe and Midnight look his way in surprise.

'*That's my pie!*' barked George. '*I was saving that!*'

Midnight – who seemed to understand George's barks – quickly put down the plate on the kitchen table, and raised his hands in surrender.

'Sorry, George,' he said. 'My bad.'

Gabe, on the other hand, strode across and flung open the cottage door.

'Shoo!' he bellowed. 'Go on, shoo!'

But George couldn't shoo; he had nowhere to shoo to. Instead, he did the only thing he could think to do, and shot past Gabe into the cottage.

'Aaagh!' shouted Gabe in surprise.

'Don't bite!' shrieked Midnight, holding up his hands. 'I've got no fur and it will really hurt!'

His heart thumping, George took it all in: the Moroccan rug, his father's velvet armchair, the battered leather sofa, the wooden kitchen table; all the things that made him feel happy and secure, though he hadn't known quite how happy and secure until this very moment.

'*Dad, it's me!*' he barked. '*It's me, George!*'

'I tried to tell him,' replied Midnight guiltily. 'But he wouldn't listen.'

'Out!' shouted Gabe to George, circling behind him. 'Get out of my house! What is going *on* tonight?'

Gabe lunged for George, and once again, everything slowed down. His dad's movements became deliberate and predictable, and George surged past him, heading for his bedroom. Midnight was standing in the way, forcing George to swerve. One of his back feet struck the base of a lamp, and it came slowly crashing down, its bright bulb exploding in a shower of sparks!

With George distracted, Gabe had just enough time to lunge forward and grab him by the collar.

They were back in real time and George could hardly breathe!

'*Dad, let go!*' he howled. '*It's me, George! Don't you recognize me?*'

It was agony!

By the time they reached the front door of Hill House, Gabe had dragged George all the way through the woods, up the drive, and — most uncomfortable of all – up the long flight of stone steps. He didn't let go when he rang the bell, and he still didn't let go when Clive answered the door.

'Oh,' said Clive, wrapping his orange dressing gown around him. 'Hello, Midnight.'

'He's been down at the cottage, barking his head off,' explained Gabe. 'I think the move's confused him.'

'Dogs, eh?' said Clive jovially. 'They're a mystery, aren't they?' He crouched down and stared right into George's eyes. 'I mean: what on earth is going on in those tiny brains of theirs?'

'Like I say,' said Gabe with a tight smile. 'I think he got lost.'

'No problem-o,' said Clive, standing aside and pulling George into the house. 'No problem-o whatsoever-o.'

Gabe nodded, and much to George's relief, finally let go of his collar.

'Oh,' Clive added. 'While I've got you – about the fishing . . .'

'Yes?' asked Gabe.

'The lake's closed, I know. But how's about I give you fifty pounds . . .' suggested Clive sleazily. 'And you let me have a crack at Gogmagog.'

Gabe narrowed his eyes.

'You drive a hard bargain, Mr Oates. Very well . . . fifty-five,' said Clive. As he spoke, he plucked two crisp bank notes from his wallet, and tucked them in Gabe's top pocket. 'Just between you and me,' he said with a wink.

There was a long pause. George – who was at just the right height to see it – saw Gabe's finger and thumb rubbing together, as if he was doing his best to control his anger.

Slowly and deliberately, Gabe took out the notes, and placed them back in Clive's pudgy hand. 'Let's pretend that didn't happen, shall we?' he said. Then he turned and made his way down the stone steps, past the fountain, and out on to the drive.

Clive closed the door, wiped his slippers on the mat, then beamed George a smile.

'Come here, Midnight,' he said, patting his knees.

George trotted forward.

OUCH!

Clive tapped him sharply on the nose!

George almost fainted with shock. It hurt more than anything had hurt in his whole life, including the time he fell out of the big apple tree and broke his arm – a mixture of brain freeze and a wasp sting. His eyes flooded with tears, and his whole head ached instantly.

'Stop running off!' spat Clive.

George tried to speak, but all that came out was a whimper.

'Look at your paws; they're filthy! There's no way you're sleeping on our bed tonight. Come on.'

Off went Clive's slippers, dragging and scraping across the hall floor, leaving George no choice but to follow them. To make matters worse, Clive's feet were really stinky, and by the time they reached the kitchen, George was ready to retch. The downside of his nasal superpowers, he decided, was that he could actually smell the black bits under Clive's yellow toenails.

Clive urged George on ahead into the boot room, whose tiles smelled so strongly of disinfectant they just about drowned out the revolting feet. The lights went out, the boot room door closed behind him, and George found himself alone.

Wait . . . was this where he was going to spend the night?

George sniffed around. No food. Just a dog bed and a bowl of water.

Lady Jane entered the kitchen and George's ears pricked up. Maybe she'd give him something to eat? He scratched at the door, but neither Clive nor Lady Jane seemed to notice.

'*Can anyone hear me?*' he whined.

The keyhole was large, and if he angled his head just right, he could see Clive, sitting at the kitchen table.

'Clarence called,' said Clive. 'He might be passing by tomorrow.'

'Your assistant Clarence?' replied Lady Jane. 'Oh that's nice for you.'

The toaster popped, the fridge rattled open, and George heard the scratch-and-slide of a knife spreading butter; butter which promptly melted, its delicious aroma wafting through the keyhole and straight into George's eager nostrils. Hot buttered toast: his favourite bedtime snack!

'Shall I ask if he wants to stay the night?' asked Clive.

'Absolutely,' replied Lady Jane.

Her heels clicked on the stone floor as she walked, and George sat up straight, ears forward, tail wagging, mouth watering, sure that the door was about to open any moment!

Then the kitchen light went off, its door swung shut, and Lady Jane and Clive's footsteps went *swish-scrape-trip-trap* off down the passage to the hall, taking the hot buttered toast with them.

George sighed deeply, and lay down with his head on the floor.

It was going to be a long night.

It was going to be a long night

CHAPTER TWELVE

'George? I've got a surprise for you.'

He was having that dream again; the one where his mum gave him Snowball.

'Close your eyes and hold out your hands.'

But this time, instead of the scratch of tiny claws, he felt the warmth of powder-soft skin.

'You can look now.'

It was a baby! A miniature, pink, human baby

wearing a nappy! A baby with dark hair and brown eyes, just like his own.

'What are you going to call him?' asked his mum.

The baby scrunched up its face, clenched its fists, and began to bawl. It began to sprout black fur, growing ears and a snout, taking the shape of a little black puppy!

'Midnight,' said a voice. 'Midnight?'

George woke to see the blurry outline of Lady Jane.

'Time for wee-wees.'

He blinked in confusion. Then it all came flooding back: the body swap with Midnight, his dad not recognizing him, the night in the boot room . . .

He pushed himself up on to all fours, and shook himself down. His ears pricked, his hackles rose, and a wave of anxiety rushed up from his tail to his neck, ending in a jaw-cracking, tooth-baring, gut-wrenching yawn! He was still a dog!

'*Lady Jane!*' he barked. '*It's me, George!*'

'And a very good morning to you too, sleepy head.' She grinned, not understanding his worry in the slightest.

'*I'm not tired!*' snapped George. '*I'm stressed!*'

'I love you too,' said Lady Jane, kneeling down and giving him a big hug. Then before he knew what was happening, she steered him out of the back door, shutting it behind him.

George stood in the cold morning air, panting. This was hopeless; he had to find Koko and reverse the spell.

'*Please!*' he whined. '*Let me in!*'

But there was no answer from Lady Jane. He could hear her clear as day, pottering in the kitchen making tea. But she couldn't hear him.

Was this how dogs spent their lives, forever

waiting for some human or other to open a door?

He tried barking, but again there was no response, so he ran around to the front door, reared up on his hind legs, and pressed the bell with his paw.

'I'll get it!' he heard Clive cry, creaking down the stairs.

Thinking quickly, George hid behind one of the two bay trees that stood either side of the porch.

Clive unbolted the outer door and popped his head out.

'Oh,' he said, seeing there was no one there. Puzzled, he edged out on to the uppermost step. As he did, George slipped silently past him and into the house.

'Hello?' called Clive, looking up and down the drive.

But George was already at the top of the stairs, sneaking past Lady Jane's open bedroom doorway and crossing the landing to Koko's room. Her door was slightly ajar, and softly and silently, he nosed his way in.

The curtains were drawn, and Koko was lying in bed, fast asleep.

George padded over and gave her hand a lick.

Koko opened one eye. 'Go away,' she said, rolling over so that her back was facing him.

George prodded her with his nose. She ignored him.

He had to tell her what happened, but how? He caught sight of Koko's desk, and padded over to it, sniffing keenly. A plate with cake crumbs – lemon drizzle, if he wasn't mistaken – a pair of binoculars and, *Ah, yes!* School things. He dragged a notebook off the desk and on to the floor, pawing it open. Then he went back for a pen, gripped it in his teeth, and started to write.

But it was useless: he couldn't see the paper. When he stepped back to take a look, all he could see was a meaningless squiggle.

There had to be another way . . .

There on a nearby shelf was a familiar-looking yellow bag: Bananagrams!

The only problem was the zip; it really wasn't meant for someone with paws instead of fingers. Luckily the bag had a little brown loop at one end, made to look like a banana stalk. After a few attempts, George was able to pin it down with his paw, then use his teeth to drag back the zip. Once enough of it was open, he gripped the other end of the bag in his teeth and shook it until the letters fell out on to the wooden floor.

Now he was facing another problem: some of

the letters had fallen upside down, and without hands it was almost impossible to turn them over.

It was going to have to be a short message.

Bit by bit, he found the letters he needed and nudged them into place with his nose.

Finishing up, he gripped the edge of Koko's duvet tightly between his teeth, braced himself, then raced across the room, pulling it completely off the bed.

Koko woke with a jump.

'Hey!' she yelled. 'What's going on?'

'*Look!*' barked George, bouncing over to the Bananagram letters, and pointing at the message with his nose. '*I left you a message!*'

'Midnight!' Koko scowled. 'Leave my stuff alone!'

And without another word she huffed over, scooped all the pieces up, and dumped them back in the bag. Then she stashed the bag on the highest shelf she could find, flung the duvet on the bed, and dived back under it.

Within seconds she was snoring.

There was only one option left: he had to talk to Midnight.

CHAPTER THIRTEEN

George's first obstacle was the front door of Hill House. Clive had closed it, so he reared up on his hind legs and released the latch. Standing on the top step, he looked out across the front lawn, the drive and the woods. Or rather, smelled out: the view was a dog's eye sludge of blue, yellow and grey; but the odours that curled at his nostrils were pin sharp. For the first time, he noticed that he didn't need to breathe in to smell something, like humans did; instead his nose was always on the go: sniffing, sampling, and discovering.

And what was that exquisite aroma, playing on the breeze? George drank it in: a deep, earthy scent that stirred feelings of excitement, interest and awe. He had to find it! Down the steps he trotted, and out on to the dewy lawn, turning this way and that, zeroing in on his target. There! He bowed his head, closed his eyes, and took a deep sniff. *Of course!* He nodded. *Badger poo.*

He was just about to roll in it, when he heard Gabe's buggy rattling off through the woods. George sprang to attention, ears forward, tail raised. His dad was off to check the fences, and riding the buggy was one of George's favourite things in the whole world, especially as Gabe sometimes let him drive.

'*Dad!*' George barked, chasing after him. '*Wait for me!*'

But by the time George reached the trees, Gabe was long gone.

Right, thought George. *Enough of being ignored.*

Moments later he was barking at the door of the cottage.

'*Open up!*' he demanded. '*It's me, George!*'

No answer. On the other side of the door, George could hear eating noises.

'*Midnight!*' barked George. '*Open the door!*'

The eating noises stopped, then started again.

'*Stop ignoring me! I know you're in there!*'

There was the sound of a sigh, then Midnight opened the door, his mouth crammed full of what smelled to George like steak and kidney pie. Every food cupboard was open, there were packets all over the floor, and the fridge was practically empty.

'George,' said Midnight casually between chews, and a little cloud of puff pastry took to the breeze. 'How's it going?'

'*What are you doing?*' barked George.

'Eating,' replied Midnight, swallowing hard. 'What does it look like?'

'*You can't just eat all the food!*'

'Yes I can. Watch.'

Midnight ripped open a packet of jam tarts and stuffed three of them in his mouth, one after another!

'*It's a complete mess in here! Dad's going to be really cross!*'

Midnight looked at the rubbish on the floor as if he was seeing it for the first time.

'*We need to tidy up,*' said George, picking up an empty crisp packet in his mouth, and laying it beside the bin. '*Come on, I'll help you.*'

'Sorry,' said Midnight through a mouthful of jam tart. 'I got a bit carried away.'

'*That's okay,*' said George. '*But being human isn't like being a dog. You can't just do what you want.*'

'Got it,' said Midnight, disposing of the empty crisp packet.

George felt his tail relax. '*At least you understand me,*' he snuffed. '*None of the humans can.*'

'Weird, isn't it?' agreed Midnight, as the two of them set to work clearing up the kitchen. 'Dogs understand everything humans do and say, but humans don't have the first clue about dogs.'

'*That's why we need to reverse the spell,*' barked George. '*So I can warn Lady Jane about Clive.*'

'Right,' replied Midnight. There was an awkward look in his eye.

'*He's a criminal, isn't he?*' barked George. '*That's why he stole those jewels.*'

'Sorry,' said Midnight, his face flushing. 'I can't get involved.'

'*What's he planning?*'

'George!' Midnight slammed the bin shut. 'Clive is my master. Good, bad, it's none of my business.'

'*Of course it's your business!*' barked George, his tail stiffening once again. '*He's up to something, and we need to find out what!*'

'No, George,' replied Midnight. '*You* need to find out. *I* need to be a faithful companion.'

There was a pause, while George considered his options. '*Fine,*' he barked. '*I want my body back.*'

'What? Now?'

'*Yes!*' George felt his ears flattening. '*Right now.*'

'Okay,' replied Midnight slowly. He paused. 'You don't want to enjoy it a bit first?'

'*Enjoy it?*' snapped George. '*My whole family are in danger!*'

'Are they though?' asked Midnight. 'Are you sure you're not getting things a little bit out of proportion?'

George grunted.

'Come on, George, this is the chance of a lifetime! You get to find out what it's like to be a dog, and I get to find out what it's like to be human! Have you ever had a tummy tickle? It feels amazing.'

'*Not as such, no,*' admitted George.

'Come on, lie down,' said Midnight. 'Right, now roll over on to your back.'

'*I don't want to.*'

'Giddy-widdy!' As he spoke, Midnight ruffled the hair on George's chest, and George felt a wave of pleasure snake down his spine and rattle his tail.

'*Stop it,*' said George, half hoping Midnight would do the opposite.

'See you on the other side, brother.'

Exactly what happened next, George wasn't sure: electric currents seemed to race around his body, filling the room with twinkling stars. Then just when he couldn't take any more, Midnight stopped tickling, and he found himself flat on his back with all four legs in the air, his mouth wide open in an enormous silent laugh!

'You see!' Midnight chuckled. 'You've got a lot to learn about being a dog! Seriously, this would be really good for you!'

George panted heavily, trying to catch his breath.

'I get it,' he spluttered, pulling himself back together. *'I love dogs, and I've always wondered what it would be like to be one. The smells, for a start. I'll never forget those, as long as I live. And chasing the stick — that was a moment. But I have to find out what Clive's up to,*

and there's no way I can do that with a body like this.'

Midnight nodded slowly, then headed for the door.

'Come on then.'

'*Where are we going?*'

'To the fountain.' Midnight smiled. 'I can see you're not happy. So we're going to change back. You see, that's a dog for you. Team player.'

CHAPTER FOURTEEN

'So,' said Midnight when they reached the fountain. 'Body-swap time.'

There was no sign of Clive. Gabe was back from his rounds, and he and Lady Jane were a safe distance away, over in the kitchen garden.

'Come on then, George, work your magic. At least I'll get two breakfasts once we switch back,' said Midnight.

'*I can't, remember?*' barked George, raising one of

his paws. *'I've got no hands and I can't speak.'*

'Good point,' agreed Midnight. 'Weird how we humans always forget that.'

'We humans?' echoed George.

'Temporary humans,' corrected Midnight. 'So come on then – what do I need to do?'

'Okay,' answered George. *'First, swirl the water anticlockwise with your hand.'*

'Like this?' asked Midnight, stirring the surface.

'Perfect,' yapped George. *'Then say the magic words: "Gogmagog, Gogmagog, Gogmagog, Gogmagog."'*

Midnight did as he was told.

'Then we both drink,' instructed George. He leaned forward and lapped the water; it really was sweet and clear, just like the spell said.

'Great,' said Midnight, cupping his hand and taking a sip. 'And what happens now?'

'We fall into a deep sleep,' grunted George,

flopping down with his head between his paws.

'Got it,' said Midnight, taking a seat beside him.

They closed their eyes.

A woodpecker drilled, a squirrel scampered across the lawn, and the sun peeped its head over the roof of Hill House, bathing them both in sunshine.

'It hasn't worked, has it?' asked Midnight matter-of-factly.

George opened his eyes and craned his neck, checking himself over. He was still covered in black fur, had an enormous bushy tail and four giant paws.

'*Maybe we should try again?*' he grunted.

Once again Midnight stirred the water, said the magic words, and they both drank. But nothing happened.

'Is it definitely "Gogmagog" four times?' questioned Midnight.

'*Yes,*' insisted George, his frustration bubbling up into anger. He began to recite:

Should a charmer take two creatures
Then stir the water round the moon.

Call his name, three times repeat it
One drop of water each consume.

'Wait a second,' said Midnight. 'Did you say *moon?*'

There was a long pause.

'So . . .' said Midnight tactfully. 'It needs to be night-time, right? So that the moon's reflected in the water?'

'*I guess,*' huffed George, not wanting to admit his mistake.

'Bummer,' said Midnight. 'We're going to have to wait till it's dark.'

George took a deep breath and sighed. Midnight ruffled the fur on the back of his head, trying to cheer him up.

'Come on, a day as a dog? Is that the worst thing ever?'

'*Maybe not*,' grunted George.

'Tummy tickle?' suggested Midnight.

'*Go on then*,' replied George, rolling over on to his back.

'Who's a clever boy then?' asked Midnight in a silly voice, as George wriggled and writhed in delight. 'Who's a clever boy? I mean, not you, obviously,' he teased. 'Because you didn't realize it had to be night-time for the spell to work.'

George's ears pricked up.

'Joke,' said Midnight defensively.

'*Wait!*' growled George. '*I can hear something.*'

'You see?' said Midnight. 'That's the other great

thing about being a dog. Top-of-the-range hearing. I swear I can hear Clive floss his teeth at night, all the way from the boot room.'

'*There's a car coming!*' barked George, feeling a sudden surge of adrenaline. '*Quick, hide!*'

Sure enough, a bright-gold open-topped mini was racing up the drive, its bonnet gleaming in the sunshine, blasting out high-energy dance music. As quickly as they dared, Midnight and George ran to the hedge, jumped it, and ducked behind it.

The car swept past them and slid to a dramatic halt, kicking up an enormous cloud of dust. As the haze cleared, they saw a handsome brown-skinned young man with short curly bleached-blond hair, sitting in the driver's seat, nodding his head in time with the music. The man cut the engine and leaped out, throwing a tan leather holdall over his shoulder. He put his hand on his hip and looked around him, taking in Hill House, the lawn, the parkland and the woods. Giving an appreciative whistle, he took off his sunglasses and wiped them clean on his sleek-looking olive boiler suit.

A voice called from behind him.

'Clarence!' Clive was bounding down the front steps. 'How kind of you to drop in!'

'Nice work, Clive!' Clarence gasped. 'Some place you've got here!'

Clive bowed his head with fake modesty. 'I really mustn't grumble, Clarence. Spacious grounds — I'm thinking: *housing estate* — and dozens of priceless antiques. I'm on to a good thing here. A *very* good thing. But wait till you see the most exciting bit.'

'Don't tell me there's a gym?'

'No. The fountain.'

Behind the hedge, George and Midnight shared a look.

'You call that a fountain?' asked Clarence, turning his nose up. 'It's tiny. Where are the stone fishes, the cherubs, the spouting jets of water? It's just a boring old bowl.'

'The correct word is *basin*,' clipped Clive. 'And it's very old.' He ran his hand along the smooth stone, smiling fondly. 'Ancient, in fact. And it's going to make us our fortunes!'

'You've already made your fortune,' said Clarence with a wicked smile.

'What, the jewels?' snorted Clive. 'That's nothing. I'm talking real money.'

'Speaking of which,' Clarence winked. 'Hand it over.'

Clive frowned.

'Clarence, please. Remember where you are.

All in good time, my friend; all in good time. I've got a master plan to turn this place into a goldmine, but we can't raise suspicion. Now, come and meet the mistress of the house.'

George and Midnight heard footsteps on the gravel, and they raised their heads over the hedge to see Clive leading Clarence in the direction of Gabe and Lady Jane.

'*Well?*' gruffed George, as soon as the two men were out of earshot. '*Now do you believe me about Clive?*'

Midnight shrugged. 'Maybe something dodgy happened on the cruise,' he said grudgingly. 'Maybe it didn't. I was eating my weight in bone marrow at Clive's sister's place, so I wouldn't know.'

'*Midnight! He's your master! Surely you care if he's a good guy or not?*'

'With respect,' said Midnight. 'We're going over

old ground. It's not my job to pass judgement.'

George could see there was no point arguing; Midnight's loyalty to Clive was beyond sense.

'*Come on,*' he grunted. '*Let's go and find Koko.*'

After trying her bedroom, the kitchen, and the orangery, George and Midnight eventually found Koko up on the hilltop behind the house, sitting on the rope swing.

'George!' she said. 'Shouldn't you be working? You know how strict your dad is.'

'I'm not George,' said Midnight, pointing to the dog beside him. 'This is.'

Koko sighed. 'Not this again. You're kidding me, right?'

Midnight shook his head. 'No, Koko. I'm not.'

Koko narrowed her eyes disbelievingly. 'So

you're telling me the spell actually worked? You've switched places?'

'One hundred per cent.'

'So you're Midnight. And that dog is George.'

'Precisely.'

Koko took out her notebook and pen, poised for action.

'All right then: tell me, Midnight, where did we first meet?'

'At the port, when your ship arrived,' came the immediate reply. 'I'd been staying with Clive's sister in Portsmouth, and she brought me to meet you.'

Koko nodded, and scribbled in her notebook.

'What was I wearing?' she asked.

'Yellow dungarees.'

Koko made a game show buzzer noise. 'Wrong. They were red.'

'Really?' asked Midnight. 'They looked yellow to me.'

George barked.

'Good point, George,' said Midnight. 'Thanks for reminding me.' He turned to Koko. 'Dogs can't see red. To us, red things look yellow.'

'Okay,' said Koko, writing it all down. 'So, George. Your turn. Yesterday, when we were in the catacomb, you told me your mum gave you something just before she died. What was it?'

George barked twice, and wagged his tail.

'An albino chihuahua puppy,' translated Midnight.

'Very good,' said Koko. 'Now write its name in the dirt with your paw.'

'Clever,' acknowledged Midnight. 'You want to make sure he's really saying something when he barks, rather than me just pretending.'

'Exactly,' agreed Koko.

'Go on, George,' urged Midnight. 'Write the name.'

But the ground by the swing was so hard and dry George couldn't even scratch it. Instead, he barked an instruction at Midnight, and went trotting down the hill, his tail high in the air.

'He says he's got a better idea,' explained Midnight. 'And we need to follow him.'

Back in Koko's bedroom, George barked again.

'He said please would you get the bag of Bananagrams down, and spread them face up on the floor?' translated Midnight.

Koko did as she was asked. Then she and Midnight waited patiently on the little sofa while George stood with his back to them, nosing the letters into place.

'Do you need some help?' asked Midnight. 'I know how difficult this stuff is without hands.'

'Uh-uh,' insisted Koko, holding Midnight back. 'He has to do it on his own.'

But when George stepped aside, all Koko could see was a jumble of letters.

'I knew it!' she said. 'You were tricking me!'

George barked.

'You're looking in the wrong place!' translated Midnight. 'It's here!'

Koko looked to where George was standing. Sure enough, between his two front paws was a word she immediately recognized, its pale tiles standing out starkly against the dark wooden floorboards:

Koko gave a sharp intake of breath.

'Is that the right answer?' asked Midnight.

Koko nodded.

'Told you,' said Midnight triumphantly. 'He's George, and I'm Midnight.'

'George!' cried Koko, throwing her arms around the dog's neck. 'I'm so sorry I didn't believe you. We have to get you guys switched back.'

George gave a single short bark.

'What did he say?' asked Koko impatiently.

'We have to wait until the moon's up,' said Midnight. 'But in the meantime, we need to find out what Clive and Clarence are up to. He says, no offence, but he doesn't trust Clive one bit.'

'Seriously? He said all that with one bark?'

'It's not just the bark,' explained Midnight. 'It's the tail, the ears, the teeth; the whole body language.'

'Impressive,' said Koko. 'In that case . . .'

She stowed her notebook, bounced off the sofa, and snatched up her binoculars.

'We've got some spying to do.'

CHAPTER FIFTEEN

'What are they doing?' mused Koko, peering through the binoculars. 'They've been talking for ages.'

The four grown-ups were in the vegetable garden, chatting, and the three friends had been watching them from the safety of the attic window.

'Greeting one another,' explained Midnight. 'That's humans for you. They take ages to say hello and even longer to say goodbye. Dogs are so much more efficient: nose-sniff, bum-sniff, bow, ready to play.'

'*Ssh*,' said Koko, raising the binoculars again. 'The targets are on the move!'

George, who had been lying on the rug, sat up straight, ears pricked. Koko watched as Lady Jane and Gabe waved goodbye, and Clive and Clarence headed off across the lawn towards the house, heads bent towards each other, deep in conversation.

'What do you think?' asked Koko, handing the binoculars to Midnight. 'Does that look suspicious to you?'

'Not really,' replied Midnight, handing them back. 'Looks like they're just chatting.'

George barked.

'What's he saying?' asked Koko.

Midnight looked shifty. 'He told me to stop defending Clive.'

Koko nodded and raised the binoculars, focusing all her attention on the magician and his assistant.

'I think they're looking to see if they're being watched. Now they're changing direction and heading towards the garage.'

George barked.

'George says we'll get a better view from the other window,' translated Midnight.

But by the time Koko and Midnight had moved the chairs they had been standing on, and climbed back up, Clive and Clarence were nowhere to be seen.

'Look,' said Koko. 'The garage door is open. They must be inside.' She adjusted the focus of the binoculars. 'Yes! I can see them, through the window. I think . . . Wait, Clive has got one of my mum's old fishing rods. Looks like they're going fishing.'

George gave a string of barks.

'Really?' asked Midnight.

'What's he saying?' asked Koko.

'He says it's closed. The lake, that is.'

'Maybe that's why they're being so secretive,' said Koko.

As she spoke, Clive peered out of the garage door to check he wasn't being watched. Then he snuck out, beckoning Clarence to follow. Clive was carrying the fishing rod, and Clarence had a tackle bag slung over his shoulder. They were heading towards the house.

'I know what they're doing!' exclaimed Koko. 'They want to catch Gogmagog.'

'Hardly the crime of the century, is it?' offered Midnight.

George barked a solitary bark.

'Fine,' replied Midnight. 'Have it your own way.'

'What did he say?' asked Koko.

'That there must be more to it than that.'

There was a pause, while Koko chewed the inside of her lip, deep in thought. 'I really don't want to think Clive is bad,' she said. 'I mean, he and Mum just got married. But George is right. He's acting very strangely. And now there's proof that the spell works . . .'

Her voice trailed away as she peered down into the courtyard.

'Quick! They've gone in the back door,' said Koko. 'Come on, you guys, let's follow them.'

As fast as they could, they tiptoed down the twisting back staircase, which led right down to the kitchen. There was movement behind the door to the boot room, and they could hear Clive and Clarence whispering.

'George, quick,' hissed Koko. 'See if you can hear what they're saying.'

George sidled up to the keyhole and used his supersonic hearing to listen carefully to the conversation.

'So,' Clarence began. 'When are you going to tell me about this tasty proposition?'

'Sssh,' replied Clive under his breath. 'Soon as we're out of the house.'

'Oh, no!' There was genuine alarm in Clarence's voice. 'I can't wear these. No way.'

'What's wrong with them?' whispered Clive.

'Clive?' asked Clarence, as if his friend was insane. 'Look at my colourway. Olive green, camel and cream. These wellies are . . . I don't even know what colour they are. Iris?'

'Fine,' hissed Clive. 'Have mine. I'll take the waders.'

'And why are we whispering?' asked Clarence. 'Lady Jane is miles away.'

'Because there are kids everywhere,' muttered Clive. 'And you know what kids are like. Ears always flapping.'

There was the hustle and bustle of two overdressed fishermen exiting a small room, then the outside door slammed shut.

'What are we going to do?' hissed Koko. 'We can't follow them; they'll see us.'

George gave a string of rapid barks.

Koko and Midnight looked at him, then at each other.

'He said—'

'I know what he said!' whispered Koko. 'Good idea, George! Go and spy on them!'

CHAPTER SIXTEEN

'**M**idnight!' said Clive without breaking stride. 'Where have you been?'

The magician and his assistant had left the lawn behind and were strolling down the hillside, on their way to the lake. But of course it wasn't Midnight that came bounding up through the bracken; it was George.

'Clarence, you remember Midnight, don't you?'

'How could I forget?' asked Clarence, without saying hello. 'Those filthy paws ruined a perfectly good pair of linen trousers.'

The lake came into view below, its water sparkling in the summer sun.

'So come on then,' said Clarence. 'What's this proposition you keep teasing me with?'

George's ears pricked up. He edged closer to Clive, to be sure of hearing the answer.

'If I tell you,' whispered Clive, 'you cannot breathe it to a soul. Has to be between you and me.'

'I'm all ears.'

'Have you ever heard of Inter-Spiritual Transmogrification?'

Clarence shook his head.

'Inter-Spitty-Confungrifi-what?'

'The story goes, that at certain sacred springs,

it's possible for beings to exchange spirits. Swap souls, if you like.'

'Seriously?'

Clive paused and mopped the back of his neck with a crumpled-up handkerchief.

'The Castalian Spring at Delphi, that's one. Manyava Skete in the Carpathian Mountains, that's another. And some believe there was one in Ancient Britain, though it's been lost for centuries. Until now.'

Clive grinned and set off again.

'What do you mean, *until now*?' asked Clarence, hurrying after him.

'I mean that I have found it.'

'What?' snorted Clarence. 'That thing you showed me at the front of the house? It doesn't look very magical to me.'

They were nearing the ring of ancient oak trees

that stood guard at the lake's edge, and beyond the nodding bulrushes, George could see blue dragonflies dancing above the surface of the pollen-crusted water.

'Appearances can be deceptive, Clarence, as well you know. Best to whisper, by the way. Carp have fantastic hearing, by all accounts.'

Clive raised his finger to his lips, and led them along the bank to a small wooden jetty. With one eye fixed on the lake, he busied himself with the rod, tweaking here and adjusting there, until everything was to his satisfaction.

'Look,' he hissed. 'In the branches.'

There was a fallen oak tree in the water, and bubbles were breaking amongst its twisted roots.

'Here,' said Clive, offering Clarence the rod.

Clarence held out his hands and grimaced, as if he was being handed a live snake.

'See if you can land it over by that tree.'

'Are you sure?' asked Clarence. 'I've never done this before.'

'Just hold the rod back,' said Clive, guiding Clarence's hands. 'Take the guard off. Hold the line with your finger . . . And cast.'

With beginner's luck, Clarence swished the rod, and the bait went whirring out across the water, landing amongst the tree roots with a satisfying *plop*.

'Nice work,' said Clive, slipping the guard back on. 'Just don't tell Gabe.'

'Who?'

'The handsome one, in the vegetable garden. Estate manager. Grumpy old so-and-so. Holds a very bright candle for Jane, if you ask me.'

George felt his ears flatten. Clive was talking about his father.

Clive set up two stools, and he and Clarence settled down to fish.

'Honestly, the cheek. Telling me I can't fish my own lake.'

George couldn't suppress a growl, and both Clive and Clarence turned in surprise.

'What's that about?' asked Clarence.

'No idea.' Clive shrugged. 'Squirrel, maybe?'

Not wanting to give himself away, George gave a friendly pant. Clive and Clarence seemed satisfied and went back to their fishing.

'You were saying,' said Clarence, still feeling rather pleased with himself for casting the bait so cleanly. 'About the fountain.'

Clive smiled to himself. The fish might not be biting, but Clarence was definitely on the hook.

'I told you,' he said casually. 'If two creatures drink from that fountain when the moon is up – under certain conditions, that is – they can swap bodies.'

'Swap bodies?' echoed Clarence. 'Why would anyone want to do that?'

'You've never been old, have you, Clarence?' Clive smiled, pushing back his wide-brimmed leather hat. The sun was stronger than it looked, and he quickly pulled it back over his shiny forehead. 'Trust me, when you get to my age, you'd give anything to feel young again. And I'm not even old; I'm only . . .'

'Sixty?' asked Clarence.

'Forty-nine,' corrected Clive.

'Sorry,' said Clarence.

Clive sighed, and continued. 'Say, for argument's sake, one knew of a great many elderly people, all of them stinking rich. Perhaps you're a piano player in an upmarket old people's home, or a maker of luxury stair-lifts, or . . .'

'A magician on a cruise ship?'

'Exactly. What if you could give those rich, elderly people one night when they can be young again? A body-swap party, if you like. How much do you think they'd pay?'

Clarence swallowed loudly.

'A small fortune.'

'No,' disagreed Clive, shaking his head with conviction. 'A horrendously large fortune.'

'I don't understand,' said Clarence. 'Where would you get the young people to swap bodies with the old ones?'

Clive's smile broadened.

'I don't know,' he twinkled. 'Who do we know with a lot of friends in, say, the dancing profession? Who work for next to nothing on cruise ships and could do with a little something extra now and then, while they wait for their West End careers to take off?'

'Me?' asked Clarence with a look of slight alarm.

'Exactly.' Clive winked.

Clarence took a deep breath and looked Clive in the eye. 'Okay. Let me see if I've got this straight. You think the fountain is magic . . .'

'No, no, no. I *know* it is.'

'How?'

'I've tested it.'

'What do you mean?'

'Two nights ago, I swapped the souls of a budgerigar and a rabbit. Last night, I swapped them back. And tonight . . . I'm going to swap souls with you.'

Clarence frowned and shook his head. He opened his mouth to speak but suddenly jerked backwards, his eyes wide.

He threw back his head and let out a high-pitched scream!

CHAPTER SEVENTEEN

Clarence's scream rang out across the valley, echoing through the woods and reaching Koko and Midnight, who had moved to the lower branches of a lime tree to carry on spying.

'What's happening?' asked Midnight urgently.

'I can't quite make it out,' replied Koko, whose view of Clarence and Clive was obscured by one of the large oak trees that ringed the lake. 'But it doesn't sound good.'

Down at the lake, Clive clamped his hand over Clarence's mouth.

'All right! All right!' he shouted. 'It was just an idea. Body-swapping isn't for everyone. Forget I mentioned it.'

Clarence twisted his head sharply, shaking free of Clive's hand.

'The line!' he gasped. 'There's something on the line!'

Clive's eyes darted across the lake, to the roots of the oak tree. The end of the fishing line was chasing up and down in the water. Something had taken the bait!

'I can't hold it!' squealed Clarence.

'Don't let go!' hollered Clive, gripping the rod alongside his assistant. 'Whatever you do, DO NOT LET GO!'

'It's the size of a whale!' howled Clarence.

George, feeling the excitement, began to bark!

'Right, I've got the rod!' yelled Clive. 'Grab my waist!'

Clarence scrambled into position.

'All we need to do is hang on,' reassured Clive. 'It'll soon wear itself ow-wow-WOOAAAARGH!'

A gigantic fish launched itself out of the water below him! It rose up, snapping its giant jaws shut just millimetres from the edge of his nose!

'EEEEEEEEEEEEEEK!' shrieked Clarence.

But it was too late. Gogmagog the giant carp crashed back into the lake, flooding the bank with a wave of water, then flexed his tail, taking out the front two posts of the jetty. The deck tipped forward and threw Clive and Clarence head first into the swirling water!

'Help!' yelled Clive, fighting to stay afloat.

'Save us!' yelped Clarence.

There was no time to waste. George tore up the bank, round the headland, and along the drive to the corner of Hill House. By that time, Gabe, who had heard the screams, was halfway across the back lawn.

'*Man overboard!*' barked George at the top of his lungs. '*Man overboard!*'

Within moments Gabe was at his side, and the two of them were running to Clive and Clarence's rescue.

As they reached the bottom of the bank, Koko and Midnight came hurrying up behind.

'Where are they?' shouted Midnight.

'*The jetty!*' barked George. *'Follow me!'*

They arrived to find Clarence, dripping wet, trying desperately to pull Clive out of the water.

'Help!' called Clive. 'Help!'

'I've got you!' thundered Gabe, pushing Clarence out of the way and hooking his arms under Clive's armpits. He grunted and heaved, and Clive's feet broke free of the surface, surrounded by a giant pair of carp lips!

'His feet!' yelled Midnight. 'It's got his feet!'

There was a loud sucking noise, and suddenly the lips were up to Clive's knees!

'Aaargh!' screamed Clive. 'It's swallowing me alive!'

SUCK!

Now Clive was in up to his chest!

'The waders!' yelled Koko. 'Get him out of the waders!' She unhooked the straps from Clive's arms. 'Now grab hold of him and pull!'

Gabe's face clouded with effort as he pulled Clive out from his waders like a cork from a bottle!

POP!

Gogmagog swallowed the waders, and sank below the surface, water slopping over the reeds until it calmed.

Clive, lying exhausted on the grass, looked down to see he was wearing nothing but his underwear.

They all looked at one another, panting and shocked.

'Perhaps,' said Gabe, 'like I suggested in the first place, we could all agree not to fish in the lake until after the full moon?'

'Absolutely,' said Clive, glassy-eyed with fright. 'I think that's an excellent idea.'

'Good,' replied Gabe, sighing and getting to his feet. 'Now, perhaps you'd like to borrow my shirt?'

CHAPTER EIGHTEEN

Out in the middle of the lake, Clive's empty waders bobbed to the surface.

Down in the darkness, half hidden in silt, Gogmagog seethed with anger. The steel hook was still caught in his upper lip, throbbing like crazy. And as it throbbed, it magnetized the jumbled thoughts of Gogmagog's brain into a single, heartfelt desire: revenge.

The rules were clear. Gogmagog had lived in this

lake for centuries. Outside the breeding season, he was fair game. But Last Blossom of Spring until the first full moon after Midsummer — that time was his and his alone.

He had been cheated, and for the first time in his long life, very nearly captured.

He would bide his time. But somehow . . .

Somehow that nasty little man with the wide-brimmed leather hat would be made to pay.

CHAPTER NINETEEN

There is nothing like a brush with a giant carp to make you feel alive, and after his encounter with Gogmagog, Clive was jollier than ever.

'You know what, Clarence?' he announced as they approached Hill House. 'You look like a man who could do with a hot shower. We've got nine bathrooms, six with showers, so take your pick. Lunch in . . . Oh yes, my watch is broken.

Does anyone have the time?'

'No,' said Clarence bitterly. 'Funnily enough, my watch isn't working either after being taken for a swim.'

Gabe looked up, shielding his eyes from the sun.

'Round about two o'clock, I'd say.'

The sight of Lady Jane only seemed to improve Clive's mood.

'Two o'clock! Time waits for no man, eh? Not even the first angler to hook Gogmagog in the history of Hill House!'

It was the sort of joke Lady Jane usually laughed at, but she could see how upset Gabe was, so all she managed was a tight smile.

'Koko, say goodbye to George,' she clipped. 'You need to catch up with your schoolwork.'

'Same goes for you, son,' added Gabe, putting his hand on Midnight's shoulder. 'That play's not going to read itself and you slept through a lot of your study time yesterday.'

Midnight and Koko glanced at one another. They couldn't be separated now! They needed to know what George had overheard at the lake . . .

'But we need to bath Midnight,' insisted Koko, pointing at George. 'Or his coat will get tangled.'

'He was so clever,' Midnight added. 'Fetching Gabe like that. The least we can do is tidy him up.'

Lady Jane and Gabe smiled at one another; school work was important, but so was looking after pets. And besides, it made them happy to see Koko and George spending time together after so long apart.

'All right then,' conceded Lady Jane. 'You can wash him in your bathroom, Koko. But as soon as you're done, it's back to work for both of you.'

The minute Koko's door was closed and the bath tap was running, Koko and Midnight huddled around George.

'Come on then, George,' whispered Koko. 'Spill the beans.'

George gave a string of urgent barks.

'Okay, it's big,' translated Midnight. 'Clive wants to hold a body-swap party!'

'A what?' asked Koko.

George barked some more.

'With lots of old, rich people from the cruise. And he's going to charge them lots of money – like millions – to swap bodies with young people, just for one night.'

'Wow,' said Koko. 'That's really creepy. You're sure that's what he said?'

George nodded and wagged his tail.

Midnight's lips twisted with worry. Now he

knew what George had overheard, it was getting harder and harder to be Clive's loyal dog and stay out of it.

'I'm really freaked out,' said Koko. 'I mean, Clive can be a bit selfish sometimes, but this . . . This is a whole other level. No wonder he's kept it secret from Mum; she'd never agree in a million years!'

George barked again, and Midnight translated.

'He says he's sorry, Koko. He doesn't want to make trouble between your mum and Clive. But we have to tell her.'

Koko nodded. 'That's just it. Mum believes in lots of things, but not magic. We need proof.'

George gave a single bark.

'The jewels,' said Midnight.

Koko thought for a moment, then spoke straight to George. 'You're right,' she said. 'The jewels prove Clive is a criminal. But how do we find them?'

Another series of barks from George.

'We go out for the evening,' translated Midnight. 'You, me, Lady Jane and Gabe. Clive is bound to give Clarence his present. When he does, George will watch and see where Clive keeps the jewels.'

'Great idea!' said Koko. 'We can go to the cinema.'

'Or the theatre?' offered Midnight. 'The Herefordshire Players are doing a production of *A Midsummer Night's Dream*. It's had some great reviews. I read it in the paper this morning.'

'Done,' said Koko. 'Come on, George, let's do this.' She flipped a lever and the bath water came spraying out of the shower attachment.

George barked anxiously.

'He says if it's all the same to us, he'd rather not,' explained Midnight. 'I know how he feels.

We dogs hate baths. It's the soap; it's disgusting.'

Lady Jane's voice rang out from the landing. 'I can hear a lot of barking. Is everything okay?'

'Fine!' called Koko.

George tried to jump out of the tub.

'George, stop it. We have to!' hissed Koko, blocking his exit. 'It's our cover story!'

'Do you need a towel?' called Lady Jane.

'One second!' replied Koko, spraying water over George's head and back. He started to struggle, but Midnight gripped him by the collar. Before George could shake himself dry, Koko smeared sickly apple-scented shampoo all over George's coat, working it up into a thick lather.

The stench was so strong it made George retch!

'Sorry, buddy,' muttered Midnight, shaking his head. 'I feel terrible about this.'

Koko rinsed her hands, opened the door, and

Lady Jane handed her an old towel.

'Thanks,' said Koko.

Behind Koko, Lady Jane saw a boy and blob of white foam in the shape of a dog.

'I was wondering if we could go out tonight?' asked Koko. 'You, me, Gabe and Midnight. I mean, George.'

'Where to?'

'The theatre, maybe?'

'To see what?'

'*A Midsummer Night's Dream.*'

There was a pause.

'Are you feeling all right?'

'Why?'

'You've never asked to do anything like that before.'

Koko shrugged. 'Growing up, I guess.' She smiled.

'I don't think we can tonight, darling. Clive has a friend staying. Besides, Gabe and I were very clear – you two have studying to do.'

'But George is reading *A Midsummer Night's Dream* at the moment. It *is* work!'

'What's that?' said Clive's voice from further down the landing. He had twisted the end of a piece of toilet paper and was using it to dry the inside of his ear.

'Koko wants to go to the theatre with George,' explained Lady Jane. 'I said not while Clarence is here.'

'Oh, I don't mind!' declared Clarence, appearing from the opposite direction. He was wearing a fluffy white robe and had a towel wrapped around his head. He threw Clive a meaningful look.

'Exactly,' said Clive, smiling at Clarence. 'It'll give Clarence and me a chance to catch up.'

'Well . . . if you're sure?' asked Lady Jane.

Clive and Clarence most definitely were.

'In that case,' Lady Jane said with a smile, 'it's a date.'

'Thank you!' Koko beamed, giving her mum an enormous hug.

'That's really kind, Lady Jane, thank you,' added Midnight politely, turning to rinse the suds off George's hind legs.

George felt Midnight's grip loosen on his collar, and immediately leaped out of the tub, desperate to get rid of the hideous smell of the soap!

He shot past Lady Jane on to the landing, but his exit was blocked by Clive on one side, and Clarence on the other! He began to dance the same crazy dance that he had seen Midnight perform in the woods the first time they met: whirling round and round, teeth and eyes wild. This was fun!

As Clive and Clarence closed in, George spotted an open door, sprinted through it, and jumped up on to the bed.

He felt himself shudder from head to toe.

'Oi!' shouted Clive. 'Midnight, stop that!'

George was shaking himself dry, wringing out his own fur like it was a wet towel, spraying suds and soapy water all over Clarence's neatly folded clothes.

'Yuck!' exclaimed Clarence. 'That's revolting. My brushed cotton pillowcase! I brought that specially!'

Lady Jane, Midnight and Koko were helpless with laughter, but Clive's face clouded with anger.

'Bad dog,' he said to George, gripping him by his collar. 'You're going in the boot room to dry off!'

Koko and Midnight shared a look. If George was

locked up, their plan would be ruined!

'But, Mum—' protested Koko.

'Clive's right,' said Lady Jane. 'Midnight's very naughty, shaking himself off like that. Clarence's beautiful things are all covered in foam.' She was trying to look serious, but her eyes twinkled with bottled-up laughter. 'Come on, you two. If we're going to the theatre, you'd better put some smarter clothes on.'

CHAPTER TWENTY

'Clarence, look what I've got!'

George woke to the sound of Clive's far-off voice ringing up the stairwell.

He rubbed his muzzle with an enormous bear-like paw and stretched out his hind legs. How long had he been asleep?

It was hard to say. He had been so bored locked in the boot room, he must have drifted off.

He barked, but there was no answer. Something

about the way the sound bounced around the building told him that Lady Jane, Koko and Midnight must have already left for the theatre.

He sniffed the air. What was that disgusting smell? It was everywhere; a cross between rotten apples and toilet cleaner. Even his paws stank of it . . .

It was him! He still reeked of that horrendous apple shampoo. The sickly-sweet perfume drowned everything else out; for a dog, it was like wearing a blindfold.

He heard a door slam on the floor above, and the sound of two feet coming down the main staircase.

'Clive?' called Clarence's voice.

George felt his ears prick up.

'In the kitchen,' called Clive. 'I've got your present.' There was the thud of something soft and heavy; then the rattle of metal as its contents were tipped out on to the table.

George padded over to the keyhole, and peered through it to see the jewels, heaped in a pile and glinting in the evening sunlight.

'Here you go,' Clive said with a grin, singling out the gold pocket watch. 'A small token of my very great esteem.'

'It's beautiful,' said Clarence. 'Thank you. And look, the famous butterfly necklace! Whose was that again?'

'Someone very, very rich and very, very stupid,' replied Clive, popping the cork from an expensive-looking bottle of champagne. 'May I?'

'Don't mind if I do,' simpered Clarence.

'Here's to very rich, very stupid people.' Clive winked.

'Chin-chin,' replied Clarence, and they clinked glasses.

The two men burst out laughing, and George felt the hair on his neck and shoulders rise in anger. They were making fun of the people they had stolen from!

Clive topped up Clarence's glass with champagne. George sniffed at the keyhole, searching for the tang of fermented grapes. But all he could smell was apple shampoo. This was going to be a real problem . . .

'So . . . are you ready then?' suggested Clive.

'For what?' asked Clarence.

'The moon's up.'

There was a pause.

'What do you mean?'

'Let's do a body swap!' Clive grinned. 'Lady Jane's out. No irritating children to get in the way. Let's do it now!'

'Erm . . .' said Clarence hesitantly.

'Surely you're not having second thoughts?' pressed Clive. 'Clarence, this is our chance. If this works, there's no end to the money we can make! These jewels are nothing compared with the riches we'll have. You can finally start your own clothing line, get someone to entertain *you* for a change while you sail around the world. The possibilities are endless!'

'I don't want to seem rude,' said Clarence delicately. 'But are you really sure about all this?

The fountain being magic, I mean?'

'Have I ever been wrong before?'

'Yes,' said Clarence. 'Lots of times. You're always losing your wand. You locked me in the box during the middle of the sword trick. And halfway through our knife-throwing act you threw a flaming machete that set fire to my trousers.'

'This is different, though!' appealed Clive. 'This isn't a trick; it's *real* magic. You saw Gogmagog. You think fish like that grow in normal lakes? Of course not. And you saw the vegetables in the garden! Giants, all of them. It's all here, look, in *The Book of Shadows.*' As he spoke, Clive flicked through the same book George and Koko had seen in the catacomb. 'This place is steeped in magic, Clarence; ancient, ancient magic. You feel it; I know you do.'

There was a pause, as Clarence scanned one of

the pages. When he looked up, something in his face had changed.

'All right, I believe you,' said Clarence. 'About the fountain being magic. But if it's all the same to you, I'd rather not swap bodies.'

'What?' spluttered Clive. 'Are you out of your mind? Why not?'

'I just don't want to. So thanks for the champagne, and the pocket watch, but I think I might head up to bed.'

'No,' insisted Clive, pushing back his chair. 'You're my assistant. You have to help me!'

'Clive, you're blocking me,' said Clarence calmly. 'Out of my way, please.'

But Clive didn't move.

'Fine,' said Clarence, 'I'll go this way.'

George backed away from the boot room door, just in time for it to open.

'Wait!' urged Clive, catching hold of Clarence's elbow, who stopped in his tracks, glowered, then turned.

'Clive,' he said firmly. 'This is your first and final warning. Let go.'

'Clarence, please!' pleaded Clive, taking hold of Clarence's hands.

'I'm not lending you my body!'

'But why?' demanded Clive. 'You have to give me a reason!'

'Because you won't look after it!'

Clive's eyes widened as Clarence's words hit home.

'Don't be silly!' Clive sputtered. 'Of course I will!'

'No, Clive, you won't,' levelled Clarence. 'You don't eat anything healthy, ever; your clothes are frankly horrible . . . I'm not sure you even clean your teeth!'

'Yes I do!' replied Clive indignantly.

'Morning and night?'

There was a pause.

'Most of them, yes . . .'

'They're yellow, Clive,' clipped Clarence, opening the back door ready for his exit. 'Your breath stinks, your eyes are puffy, and under that hat, you're bald!'

'Not completely!' protested Clive. 'I've got bits at the sides!'

'That's not hair, Clive . . . It looks like the fluff you find in a Hoover bag.'

'Clarence, this is a huge opportunity,' begged Clive. 'Huge.'

'I don't care,' said Clarence, folding his arms and standing tall. 'I'm not doing it.'

'What if I gave you *all* the jewels?'

There was a long pause.

'Seriously?' asked Clarence.

Without saying another word, Clive marched to the kitchen table, scooped up the jewels, and stuffed them into the purple velvet bag. He held it out, offering it to Clarence.

'Here,' he said.

'You're *giving* me all the jewels?' asked Clarence in disbelief.

Clive nodded. 'On condition that you body-swap with me right now.'

Clarence narrowed his eyes. 'For how long?'

'One hour.'

Clive held out his hand for Clarence to shake.

'Deal?'

'No crisps?' questioned Clarence. 'Or junk food of any kind?'

'I swear,' said Clive.

Clarence stared at Clive's outstretched hand, then at the purple bag. A slow smile spread across his face and he shook.

'Yes, Clive, I'll body-swap with you. Deal.'

Clive and Clarence eyeballed one another warily, before Clarence broke the silence.

'I'm going to go and put this somewhere safe,' he said, raising the purple velvet bag that held the jewels.

'You do that,' said Clive, tipping his wide-brimmed leather hat. 'I'll see you by the fountain.'

This is my chance, thought George. *I have to see where Clarence hides the jewels!*

He tried to follow Clarence down the passage, but with his nose still full of apple shampoo, it was almost impossible! Doggy eyesight really was very blurry close up. By the time he reached the hall, he needed a new plan. So instead of following

Clarence's scent up the stairs, he skidded across the polished wooden floor and out through the open front door, feeling the breeze of the great outdoors. Knowing he had only moments to spare, he pattered down the steps, and out on to the lawn, searching for . . . searching for . . . what exactly?

Yes! A deliciously musky scent, nestling in the grass. The badger poo! It wasn't quite the same as his own smell, but it was close enough. He rolled over on to his back and wriggled up and down, trying to get as much of it as he could on to his foul soap-smelling body!

He gave his back a quick sniff. It wasn't perfect, but it would have to do. Then he sampled the air. Finally, everything came into focus around him: the ferns in the woods, the daisies on the lawn, even the spider webs in the box hedges. He was ready for action.

Except . . . Clive was heading down the steps towards him! He needed to keep out of sight, in case he was shut in again. Thinking quickly, he raced round to the open back door. Then he tore through the boot room, hung a right in the hall, pelted up the stairs to Clarence's room, and slipped in through the open door.

Clarence was standing with his back to him, holding the purple velvet bag.

He moved over to a chair, picked up his tan leather holdall, and tucked the jewels inside. Smiling to himself, he reached up and put the bag on top of the wardrobe. He was turning back to the door when he caught sight of George and jumped in surprise.

'Aaagh!' he shouted.

'*Aaagh!*' replied George. But of course, like everything else George tried to say, it came out as a bark.

'You've got a nerve,' said Clarence, narrowing his eyes. 'Thanks to you, this jumpsuit is all I've got to wear.'

George panted.

'EEEEW,' said Clarence. 'What's that smell?' He screwed up his face in displeasure, flaring his nostrils. 'Is that . . . poo?'

George lay down on the rug, as if he had no idea what Clarence was saying.

'Eurgghh! Disgusting!' exclaimed Clarence. 'Out! Out!'

He shooed George out of the door, closing it carefully behind them.

Keeping his distance, George followed Clarence out of the front door and down the stone steps.

The nearly round moon was rising and the trees on the lawn were casting long shadows in the moonlight.

Clive was waiting patiently by the fountain.

'What do I have to do?' asked Clarence reluctantly.

'Nothing,' replied Clive. 'I've already said the enchantment. All you have to do is drink this water.'

Clive brandished two empty champagne glasses, scooped them in the water, and offered one to Clarence.

'Bottoms up,' said Clive. With a glint in his eye, he knocked back the entire glass, his Adam's apple bouncing with loud gurgling gulps.

Clarence eyed his glass as if he might be having second thoughts. But then he shrugged, leaned forward and took a delicate sip.

'One drop is all it takes.' Clive smiled, setting the two glasses down beside the fountain. 'Feeling anything yet?' he asked.

Clarence shrugged. 'A bit tired,' he murmured, eyes half closing. Then without another word, his head lolled forward and he keeled over on to the gravel, fast asleep.

Clive's eyes widened in anticipation. 'It's working,' he muttered excitedly. He looked up at the moon, framed between wisps of cloud. Settling himself back against the fountain, he smiled and closed his eyes.

There was the sound of a car approaching, and a pair of bright headlights swept across the front of the house. Clive's eyes slowly reopened and he squinted, trying to bring the car into focus.

'Uh-oh,' he whispered. Then he keeled over too.

CHAPTER TWENTY-ONE

L ady Jane's Land Rover growled to a halt, its headlamps slicing the gloom like searchlights. Delighted, George went bounding over towards it, barking at the top of his lungs.

'Goodness me, Midnight!' exclaimed Lady Jane. She cut the engine and the lights, and jumped down from the driver's seat. 'What a welcome!'

'I'm going to head back to the cottage,' said Gabe.

'Really?' asked Lady Jane. 'I thought we were going to have ice cream?'

'I don't want to intrude,' said Gabe firmly. 'George: half an hour.'

'Thanks, Dad,' replied Midnight, as George jumped up at him, barking furiously.

'What's he saying?' hissed Koko in Midnight's ear.

'He knows where the jewels are!' came the whispered reply.

'What?' Koko's eyes shone with excitement. 'Where are they?'

'Come on, you two!' called Lady Jane from the steps.

George turned back to the fountain and saw that Clive and Clarence had vanished!

Lady Jane hoisted up a cloth bag, and dangled it invitingly. 'Let's drown our sorrows in ice cream.'

The mystery of Clive and Clarence's disappearance was soon solved, because when Lady Jane and the two children arrived in the sitting room, the magician and his assistant – or their bodies, at least – were sitting awkwardly in two armchairs.

'I'm Clive,' blurted a man that looked like Clive, the second they set foot in the door.

'I know,' said Lady Jane, slightly bemused. 'We're married, remember?'

'And that's Clarence,' he said, pointing at someone who looked just like Clarence.

George butted Midnight's hand, urgently.

'What is it?' he whispered.

'They've swapped bodies!' barked George.

Midnight tapped his nose, to show he had understood, and whispered in Koko's ear. *'Ah!'* mouthed Koko silently. Lady Jane on the other hand was completely baffled.

'Hello, darling,' said Clive, from inside Clarence's body.

Lady Jane's face fell.

'I mean, *Lady Jane*,' corrected Clive, suddenly remembering he was meant to be Clarence, and it was a bit weird for Clarence to call Lady Jane 'darling'. 'You're back early?'

'The curtain got stuck! At the interval. All we saw was the first half.' She fished a tub of ice cream out of the cloth bag. 'So I bought a whole load of these, and we came straight home. Can I tempt you, Clarence?'

She held out the bag towards the man she thought was her guest, jostling the tubs inside.

'Ooh yes please,' said Clive from inside Clarence's body, greedily fishing out a tub.

'Oh no you don't,' said the real Clarence, snatching it away. 'We had an agreement, remember?'

201

Of course, thought George. *Clarence doesn't want Clive eating junk food while he's in his body.*

'Clive!' exclaimed Lady Jane. 'What on earth are you doing, snatching away Clarence's ice cream?'

'He's not hungry,' replied Clarence from inside Clive's body, handing the ice cream back. 'He doesn't want sugar so close to bedtime.'

'Right,' said Lady Jane, confused as to why her husband was being so rude to their guest. 'Here, George, help yourself. And you, Koko. And err . . . if Clive will let me . . .' She laughed nervously. 'Hahaha, I might have one too.'

'I'll put the rest in the freezer,' offered Koko, seeing her chance to leave the room.

Lady Jane, who was still a little shaken by Clive and Clarence's odd behaviour, smiled gratefully. 'Yes, that's very helpful. Thank you, Koko.'

Koko gave a signal to Midnight and George, and

the two of them followed her out into the hall.

'So where are the jewels?' whispered Koko.

'*Follow me!*' barked George, bounding up the main staircase to Clarence's room.

As soon as Koko opened the door, he rushed inside, sniffing eagerly.

'*There!*' he barked. '*On top of the wardrobe!*'

Sure enough, there was Clarence's holdall, way up high.

'I don't understand,' said Koko. 'Why has Clarence got them?'

'*To make him do a body swap!*' barked George.

Koko stared at him blankly.

'*I'll explain later!*'

'Quick!' said Midnight. 'Koko, climb on my shoulders.'

Teetering over towards the bag, Koko reached out and tugged.

203

'Careful,' cautioned Midnight. 'We don't want to damage the jewels!'

Koko gave the bag a giant heave and down it came, bouncing off Midnight's head and narrowly missing George. As it landed they heard a deafening crash and a scream from below! Koko grabbed the holdall and the three of them rushed downstairs and skidded into the sitting room.

'Koko!' Lady Jane cried in panic, pulling at her husband's sweater. 'Help me! Quick!'

In front of the hearth was a large padded coffee table that was usually covered with art books and magazines but was now the floor of a wrestling ring, in which Clive and Clarence were locked in a desperate struggle. Beside them, a vase lay in smithereens on the soaked carpet, surrounded by a bunch of flowers, and a large bar of chocolate.

'How dare you!' croaked Clarence from inside

Clive's body. 'I *told* you not to eat any junk food.'

'Get off!' squeaked Clive, from inside Clarence.

'What happened?' asked Midnight, as he and Koko tried to pull the stout magician off his beanpole assistant.

'I have no idea!' replied Lady Jane, exasperated. 'Clarence moved on to chocolate, and the next thing I knew, Clive just flew at him!'

'Stop it, you two!' yelled Koko, trying to pull the two men apart.

'Honestly,' said Lady Jane, 'I don't know what's got into them.'

George did the only thing he could think to do: he sat fully upright, threw back his head, and howled!

It was such a strange, unexpected noise that the humans in the room instantly stopped what they were doing and turned to look at him. Clarence (from inside Clive's body) appeared to come to his senses and removed his hands from around the magician's neck.

Midnight poured a glass of water, and the fake Clarence drank it gratefully.

Once he could see that everyone was safe, George stopped howling.

'Well done, Midnight,' said Lady Jane gratefully. 'At least one of us is thinking straight. Now, will somebody please explain what on earth is going on?'

'Easy,' replied Koko, dumping the holdall on to the rug in front of Clive and Clarence. 'This!'

CHAPTER TWENTY-TWO

'Remember the necklace that lady lost?' asked Koko, triumphantly. 'On the cruise?'

'How could I forget?' replied Lady Jane. 'She tried to put the blame on Clive, of all people!'

'Well it's here,' said Koko. 'In Clarence's holdall. Along with all the other jewels Clive stole. Clive is a crook!'

There was a long pause while Lady Jane looked

from Koko to the man she thought was her husband and back again.

'You can't be serious?' she asked.

Koko turned to Clarence with a confident smile, knowing it was really Clive inside.

'Open it,' she said.

There was a slight pause, as the magician and his assistant played for time.

'Gosh, imagination is a wonderful thing,' said Clive, from inside Clarence's body. 'I'd rather not open it, though, if it's all the same to you. It's got my dirty smalls inside.'

'Clarence, I'm so sorry,' said Lady Jane, flushing with embarrassment. 'Koko, this is no way to treat a guest. I'm mortified.'

'That's okay,' said Clive and Clarence together, then looked at one another uncertainly.

'He's lying!' cried Koko. 'The jewels are in

there, I swear! And this . . .'

She pointed at the man who looked like Clarence.

'This isn't even Clarence. It's Clive. In Clarence's body!'

'What do you mean, that's Clive? Koko are you all right?' asked Lady Jane, looking very concerned.

'That's why they were fighting just now,' insisted Koko. She darted forward and – so far as Lady Jane could see – tried to wrestle the bag out of Clarence's hands.

'Koko!' said Lady Jane.

'It's true! Clive only married you because he knew the fountain was magic!'

'Koko!'

'All he cares about is money! He wants to use the magic and make millions!'

Lady Jane's face clouded. 'That's enough! What's got into you?'

209

'You have to believe me!'

'Upstairs! Now! And you can stay there until you're ready to apologize,' seethed Lady Jane as Koko burst into tears and ran from the room.

There was an awkward pause.

'It's my fault,' said Lady Jane, picking up Koko's empty ice-cream tub. 'Too much sugar.'

George slipped quietly out.

Koko was lying face down on her bed, and George could smell the damp salty whiff of tears. He nuzzled her shoulder, and she looked up.

'He's going to get away with it,' she said, shaking her head in disbelief. 'I know he is. What are we going to do?'

There was a soft knock at the door, and Lady Jane entered. 'Koko?'

'What?'

'I'm sorry I spoke to you like that.'

Koko didn't answer.

Lady Jane gave a sad little smile, and sat down on the bed.

'Clive is a good man. I hope you know that.'

Koko still didn't answer.

'It's fine to make mistakes, Koko. But when we do, it's up to us to say sorry.'

'I didn't make a mistake,' muttered Koko into her pillow.

Lady Jane sighed. When she spoke again, there was a firm tone to her voice. 'In that case, you can have an early night, and see if you feel differently in the morning. I've sent George home too, before you ask. Let's have a better day tomorrow, shall we?'

She smoothed the bedspread, got up, and closed the door.

As soon as she had gone, Koko leaned into

George's ear. 'Stay close to the real Clive,' she whispered. 'Sooner or later he'll make a mistake. When he does, we need to be there. Keep an eye on Clarence, too.'

'Midnight!'

Right on cue, a voice that sounded very much like Clive's drifted up the stairs.

'Midnight? Walkies!'

'That's Clive now,' hissed Koko. 'No wait,' she corrected herself. 'It's Clarence in Clive's body. Quick, don't let them out of your sight!'

'There you are!'

A man who looked like Clive was talking to Lady Jane. George padded towards him and panted a greeting.

'It's not true, is it, Clive?' asked Lady Jane. 'What Koko was saying?'

'Of course not, Lady Jane. I mean, darling,' said Clarence from inside Clive's body.

'You didn't steal that necklace? On the cruise?'

'Absolutely not!'

Lady Jane smiled nervously.

'Like Clive said,' continued Clarence, then hesitated, realizing his mistake. 'Wait a minute – I'm Clive!' He made a silly face, rolling his eyes. 'I mean like *Clarence* said, it's proof of an extraordinary imagination. Didn't do William Shakespeare any harm, did it? Talk about *A Midsummer Night's Dream*! If Koko can harness that, she's going to go far, I can tell you.'

Lady Jane leaned forward for a kiss, but Clarence, inside Clive's body, leaned back.

'Ooh, let's not do that just now. Clive and I . . .'

213

He corrected himself. 'I mean *Clarence* and I . . . are going to take Midnight for a walk.'

'What, now? It's bedtime.'

'He really needs a walk, don't you, boy?'

George said nothing.

'Come on,' said Lady Jane, taking the man she thought was Clive by the hand. 'You can walk Midnight in the morning.'

Her husband's eyes widened in fright.

'I can't . . . I mean, I've promised Clive . . . I mean Clarence is waiting for me outside. When we've swapped back . . . No, when we've taken Midnight for a walk, he'll be right up. Clive, that is. I mean me — I will. I'm not feeling very well — I need some fresh air. Which is why I'm taking Midnight for a walk. Because I'm Clive and Midnight is my dog. Goodnight.'

And with that he hurried across the hall and out

of the door, George following close behind him.

The real Clive was waiting for them at the fountain. Without a word to Clarence, he looked up at the almost full moon, breathed in a lungful of cold night air, then began to stir the water anticlockwise.

'Gogmagog, Gogmagog, Gogmagog, Gogmagog,' he chanted.

Lifting his hand from the water, he let a single drop roll on to his tongue. Then he sat down with his back propped against the fountain and shut his eyes. The real Clarence then copied him exactly.

There was a flash of moonlight, then silence, and George found himself guarding the sleeping bodies of his enemies.

It was Clarence that stirred first.

'Oh thank goodness!' he whispered. 'I'm me! I'm me!'

He looked sideways at Clive, who was still fast asleep. He frowned. 'Clive? Are you okay?'

But Clive wasn't moving. Concerned, Clarence sat him up straight, and patted him gently on the cheek.

'Clive,' he whispered. 'Wake up!'

Clive's eyes sprang open, and he grabbed Clarence by the collar of his expensive-looking boiler suit! George could smell his anger — it was a spicy, aggressive scent.

'Ow! Clive!' protested Clarence. 'You're hurting me! I'm sorry I tried to stop you eating that chocolate, okay?'

'Why?' insisted Clive, getting heavily to his feet. 'Why did you tell Koko about my plan?'

'No, Clive, I swear!'

'How did she know about the jewels then?' growled Clive. 'If it wasn't you, how did she know?'

With a sudden burst of strength, he pushed Clarence backwards into the water of the fountain!

George barked in alarm, gripping Clive's trouser leg and beginning to pull.

'Midnight, get off!' hissed Clive, kicking George away. 'I'll teach you to cross me, Clarence. I thought we were in this together.'

Clarence's head was hovering dangerously close to the water. In desperation, George clamped his jaws around Clive's ankle.

'Ow!' howled Clive, and Clarence burst out of the fountain, fighting to get out of the water.

'Bad dog!' snapped Clive, lashing out at George with the toe of his boot, and only narrowly missing.

'It wasn't me!' gasped Clarence. 'Please, I swear, it wasn't me!'

'Oh really? Who was it then?' shouted Clive, gripping Clarence in an extremely uncomfortable-looking headlock. 'The dog?'

'*Let him go!*' barked George.

Clive flashed an angry look at George; then, as it faded, realization bloomed. Releasing Clarence, he lunged forward and seized George by the collar!

A torch swept across them; it was Midnight, returning from the cottage.

'What's going on?' he called.

'Good question,' answered Clive, drawing himself to his full height. 'Why don't you tell me?'

CHAPTER TWENTY-THREE

As the fountain trickled, the four of them stood like statues in the moonlight.

Clive spoke first. 'Here, Midnight. Now.'

As George trotted over, continuing to play along, the boy lowered the torch. He clenched his jaw, trying hard to resist. But it was useless; he had to obey. He took a deep breath and walked slowly towards his master.

'Sit,' said Clive.

Without speaking, Midnight sat cross-legged on the gravel.

'Good boy,' said Clive, ruffling his hair. He squatted down, so that he was looking right into Midnight's eyes. 'You swapped bodies, didn't you? You and George?'

'*Don't say anything!*' barked George.

Midnight gave George a sorrowful look, then returned his attention to Clive.

'Yes,' he said, his eyes full of sadness and regret. 'George saw you do the spell, and then he copied you. Now I'm in his body, and he's in mine.'

There was movement at the top of the steps, and Lady Jane appeared in the doorway silhouetted against the bright yellowy-orange glow of the hall.

'Is everything all right?' she asked.

'I'm afraid not,' said Clive. He stood up and

pointed an accusing finger at George. 'This crazy dog pushed Clarence into the fountain, then bit me on the ankle. Look!'

As he spoke, Clive lifted his trouser leg, and shone Midnight's torch to show George's teeth marks.

'Oh my goodness!' exclaimed Lady Jane. 'Wait right there.' She turned on her heel and disappeared inside the house.

'*What are you doing?*' barked George to Midnight. '*Why did you tell him we swapped bodies?*'

'Clive's my master —' Midnight shrugged — 'I've got no choice.'

'*Of course you do!*' barked George. '*Everyone has a choice!*'

'Every human, maybe,' replied Midnight. 'But not every dog.'

'You see, Clarence?' called Clive triumphantly.

'They're talking to one another. That's how they know all our secrets.'

'If that's your apology,' huffed Clarence, massaging his neck, 'it's not accepted.'

'You attacked me for eating chocolate!' protested Clive.

'On top of an ice cream!' snapped Clarence. 'When you promised me no junk food!'

'Can everyone please stay calm?' called Lady Jane. She had reappeared at the top of the steps, and was now making her way towards them, carrying a large red first-aid box. 'I know a dog attack is extremely upsetting, but I don't want anyone going into shock.'

She clipped a lead on to George's collar, handed the other end to Clive, then took the torch and shone it on Clive's ankle. 'It's bleeding, Clive. This is quite serious. Bad dog, Midnight! Bad dog!'

'Ow!' winced Clive, playing up. 'It really hurts.'

Lady Jane swabbed the wound. 'I just don't understand it,' she said, throwing George a steely look. 'You've always been such a friendly dog. Why would you do a thing like this?'

'*I had to!*' barked George. '*He was going to drown Clarence!*'

'You see how aggressive he is?' said Clive. 'He's out of control. George saw it all, didn't you, George?'

Midnight studied his shoes.

'George?' pressed Clive. 'You saw this dog bite me, didn't you?'

Not looking up, Midnight nodded. 'Yes,' he mumbled.

George felt a pain in his heart. His tail drooped and his head hung low.

Lady Jane put the finishing touches to an elaborate dressing, then restored Clive's sock to

223

its natural habitat underneath Clive's trouser leg.

'And what about you, Clarence?' she asked, lighting him up with the torch. 'Are you all right?'

'Just about,' murmured Clarence.

'Good gracious!' exclaimed Lady Jane. 'You're soaked! Again! George,' she said, turning to Midnight, 'help Clarence up the steps; he needs another hot shower!'

Midnight gave George a final, sorrowful look, then offered his shoulder for Clarence to lean on.

'I won't forget this, Clive,' said Clarence.

He and Midnight went limping towards the house, leaving George alone with Clive and Lady Jane.

'What do we do?' Lady Jane sighed, closing the first-aid box.

'Kennels,' said Clive, tightening his grip on George's lead. 'There's no other option.'

'What sort of kennels?'

'Special ones,' reassured Clive. 'For dangerous dogs. I'll take him now. Even though it's only a small bite, I don't want to risk him doing this again – not around Koko.'

'Are you sure, Clive? This is a big decision.'

'It's for the best. Important to nip it in the bud, before he forms a habit.'

'*He's lying!*' barked George.

'You see him baring his teeth?' said Clive. 'Honestly, I don't recognize him. If I let go of him now, I don't know what he'd do.'

Lady Jane backed away, tears welling in her eyes.

'Okay,' she said bravely. 'Goodbye, Midnight. We'll see you soon. And when we do, you'll feel better. Much, much better.'

'*Don't trust him, Lady Jane!*' called George, as Clive dragged him towards the waiting Land Rover. '*He's a crook! All he cares about is money!*'

It was no use. The next thing George knew, the rear door of the Land Rover slammed shut, and Clive was sneering at him from the driver's seat.

'Dumb move, kid.' Clive grinned. 'Because you've rumbled my plan, I'm going to have to get rid of Koko and Lady Jane. And you . . . You're going to spend the rest of your life as a dog.'

He started the engine, swept around the fountain, and sped off down the drive.

CHAPTER TWENTY-FOUR

C lang!

George watched helplessly through the rear window as they clattered over the cattle grid at the main gate, and on to the highway. Clive revved the engine, the road curved, and Hill House vanished into the night.

A wave of anxiety rippled over George: his haunches lowered, his back arched, and his jaws yawned wide. There were bars between him and

Clive, so the only way out was through the rear door. A quick sniff located the handle, fresh with Clive's bitter scent. If he could only get his paw that high . . .

But it was useless. He tried pushing it, pulling it – even bending it with his teeth – but it wouldn't budge. Even if he could open the door, at the speed they were driving, there was no way he could jump without getting badly hurt. And then how would he make it back to Koko and Lady Jane?

Pressing his nose against the glass, he watched the trees rush in behind him. Then the woods fell away, and they swept on to a large open roundabout to join an enormous dual carriageway.

Cars whistled past, each one moving too fast for George to be able to attract their attention. As the road steepened, they overtook an enormous lorry, lit up like an ocean liner; its fumes were so strong they made George feel queasy. He barked at the driver, but it was no use; the engine noise completely drowned him out.

But wait! They were passing a police car, parked on a raised verge!

Could this be his chance?

The policeman glanced up, and George waved frantically.

The policeman stared back open-mouthed, dumbfounded to see a large black dog waving at him from inside a passing car.

'*Help!*' barked George. '*I've been kidnapped!*'

But it was no use; the only person to take notice was Clive.

'Don't worry, George,' he shouted. 'It is George, isn't it?'

George didn't answer.

Clive flicked on the indicator light, and they left the dual carriageway.

'I know you're thinking you might get away. That you might save Lady Jane, or get to be a boy again. But it's never going to happen.'

They paused, waiting for a traffic light.

'You see, the magic stops at midnight tomorrow.'

George felt his ears droop.

'It's all there in *The Book of Shadows*, my friend. It lasts from midnight on Midsummer's Night, till midnight on the full moon. You'd have to wait until next year, and by then Lady Jane and Koko will be long gone, your dad will be out of a job, and the fountain will belong to me.'

George listened in silence, knowing in his heart that what Clive said was true.

'If I have one wish for you, George, it's this: I hope you like dog food.'

George growled, but Clive seemed not to hear. The traffic light changed, and they pulled out on to an empty parkway lined with brightly lit car showrooms. Wherever they were, it was now a long way from Hill House.

Who could help him now? Midnight had betrayed him. Though he could imagine how hard it must be for a dog to disobey its master . . . Koko was in bed in disgrace and didn't know what had happened. Where would his dad be? In the cottage, no doubt, cooking for Midnight, mistakenly thinking Clive's dog was his son.

Koko was his best hope. Come the morning, she would find out that he was missing; then surely, she would come looking for him. But what if Clive got to her first? He *had* to escape, get back to Hill House, and warn them!

Clive suddenly slammed on the brakes and

George lurched forward, striking his nose on the bars. He just had time to make out a high brick wall topped with barbed wire before the back door sprang open and Clive yanked him out by his lead.

'You know what works best in times of great adversity, George?' asked Clive. Then without waiting for an answer, he said, 'Acceptance.'

They were in a narrow lane and up ahead was an imposing metal security gate, and a sign that he couldn't make out. George sniffed the air: it replied with the scents of a hundred dogs.

'So what does that mean in your case?' continued Clive, pulling George towards an intercom on the gate. 'I guess it means . . .' Clive paused, searching for the right words. 'Accepting that you failed and *nobody* will catch me. Hill House will be mine and I'll be a MILLIONAIRE!'

Clive looped George's lead around a bar of the

gate and tied it tight. Then he pressed the button and stood back.

'*Hello?*' said a distorted voice. '*Paws for Thought.*'

'Hi,' replied Clive. 'Got a stray dog for you. Be careful though, it's extremely dangerous. Severe case of "lock him up and throw away the key".'

Clive turned to George and made a pretend sad face.

'Poor little George. I'm going to put you out of your misery. I don't want you spending years in here, wondering what happened to Koko and Lady Jane, and whether or not you could have done anything to save them. So here's how this is going to pan out. I'm going to wait until tomorrow evening, just before midnight. Then I'm going to make Koko and Lady Jane swap bodies with my rabbit and my budgerigar. Neither of them will make much sense after that, I don't expect. I'll stick 'em somewhere out of sight, inherit the fountain, and next summer its magic will make me stinking rich. Sound like a plan?'

Rage surged in George's veins! Ears flat and teeth bared, he launched himself at Clive in the slowest of slow motion. He was just about to clamp his jaws either side of Clive's bulbous blue-veined nose when his lead was yanked tight around his neck. The world jolted back into real time, and George was left coughing and spluttering.

'*I see him,*' said the voice on the intercom. '*We've got him on camera. I'll be right out.*'

Clive smiled and shook his head, as if he couldn't quite believe how clever he was.

'You make a great audience for my tricks, George,' he said cheerily. 'You walked right into that one. Whatever I do, you always manage to stay one step behind.'

Without another word, he turned on his heel and walked towards the car.

George screwed his eyes tight and shook himself furiously, releasing all his pent-up anger. By the time he opened them again, the tail lights of the Land Rover were turning the corner at the end of the lane, and he was alone.

On the other side of the security gates, a light came on. Footsteps, rubber soles on tarmac, came squelching softly towards him. The man on the intercom was coming for him!

George panted heavily, mind racing. With one last desperate effort, he gripped the lead with his teeth and shook it hard, trying to work it free. But it was no use; he was stuck.

A bolt rattled on the other side of the door. It edged ajar, and a young man with long frizzy hair popped his head out of the gap.

'Hello there!' He grinned. 'What's your story?'

'*That man was lying!*' whined George. '*I'm not dangerous, I promise!*'

'Easy now. Easy now,' said the man kindly, as he took several slow, confident steps forward, a playful smile on his lips.

George lay down, twitching his tail.

'You look pretty friendly to me,' said the man. He held out his hand for George to sniff: it contained a folded-up slice of salami sausage so inviting that George was unable to resist wolfing it down.

'My name's Timmy,' said the man. He scratched George behind his ear, sending a shiver of warmth down his spine and into his tail, where it became an energetic wag. 'What's your name, I wonder?'

Timmy felt like someone George could trust. So when he untied George's lead and led him through the security gates, George went willingly. Soon they reached Timmy's office, where he picked up a form and began to fill it out.

A wave of tiredness washed over George and he lay down, panting.

'Easy, big fella,' said Timmy. 'Easy now. How's that sleeping tablet treating you?'

What? thought George. *Sleeping tablet?!*

Looking around, he spotted a half-eaten pizza and a bottle of pills.

Of course! The salami . . . Timmy must have wrapped a sleeping pill in it!

Then everything went black.

CHAPTER TWENTY-FIVE

Koko was in disgrace. It wasn't until late afternoon the following day that she finally caved in, and agreed to go with Lady Jane to the drawing room, where Clive and Clarence were waiting.

'So what's the plan?' Clarence whispered, as he and Clive took position at the mantelpiece. Lady Jane had told them Koko would be in any minute.

'Easy as pie,' gloated Clive. 'When Koko's apologized, we celebrate with these four glasses of cloudy lemonade. Cloudy, my dear friend, to disguise the fact that these two –' he pointed to two pink glasses, sitting beside two clear glasses on a silver tray – 'are laced with my patent knockout powder. Once they're asleep, we tie them up. Then just before midnight, we body-swap them for the budgie and the bunny.'

'What about Gabe?' asked Clarence. 'How do we take care of him?'

'We won't have to,' said Clive, with a wink. 'If he comes looking for Lady Jane – and let's face it, he's in love with her, so he probably will – we'll say she's not feeling well and she's gone to bed.'

'But . . . what if he sees us? When we take them out to the fountain?'

'Oh, Clarence,' giggled Clive, shaking his head.

'For a man who works in entertainment, you really don't know much about manipulating people, do you? That's why we wait until just before midnight. Even if he sees us, he won't have time to stop us. The clock will strike twelve and the magic will stop! Lady Jane and Koko will be animals for ever!'

There was a knock at the door, and Lady Jane and Koko entered.

'Here she is!' said Clive with relish. 'What do you have to say for yourself, young lady?'

'Well?' said Lady Jane, prompting her.

'Sorry, Clive,' said Koko, without any trace of expression. 'And sorry, Clarence.'

'Dear, dear Koko,' gushed Clive. 'I can't lie. You hurt my feelings. And you know why? Because I care about you. But all is forgiven. Perhaps we should have a little drink together?'

'Bottoms up,' said Clarence, making sure Lady

Jane took one of the two pink glasses.

'Delicious,' said Lady Jane, taking a sip.

'Koko?' offered Clarence.

'No thanks,' said Koko.

Clive frowned.

'Can I play with Midnight now?'

Clive and Lady Jane looked at one another.

'Midnight's been sent to the dogs home,' explained Lady Jane. 'There was a bit of an incident last night, after you went to bed.'

'What sort of incident?' Koko felt panicked.

'I'm so sorry,' said Clive, his voice full of regret. 'He bit me and he's going to need a little bit of rehabilitation.'

Koko's eyes narrowed. Clive was up to something, but if she lost her temper again, she'd be grounded. She needed to be cunning; as cunning as Clive himself.

'Oh no?' she said, her voice full of concern. 'Did he hurt you?'

'I'll live,' said Clive bravely. 'So. Since Midnight is unavoidably detained, perhaps you'd join us in a glass of cloudy lemonade?'

But once again, Koko didn't take the glass.

'Can I get you some arnica?' she asked sweetly. 'I've heard it's very good for cuts and bruises.'

'Very thoughtful, Koko,' said Lady Jane approvingly. 'There's some in the medicine cabinet in the boot room. I'm sure Clive would really appreciate that, wouldn't you, Clive?'

'I'd rather she just drank the lemonade,' said Clive.

'I will, I promise,' said Koko with a smile. 'As soon as I'm back.'

The second Koko was out of the room, she went tearing across the hall to the front door, where she bumped straight into Midnight!

'Koko! I've been trying to get away all day to tell you—'

'George is in the dog pound!'

'What? How did you . . . ?'

'Clive just told me. He must have found out you and George swapped bodies!'

Midnight swallowed his guilt. 'It was me, Koko. I'm so sorry.'

'You told Clive!' Koko's mouth fell open in surprise.

'I couldn't help it, Koko. He got it out of me. I have to tell him the truth – he's my master.'

'That's no excuse! What about your conscience?' jabbed Koko, indignation flashing across her face.

'I know, I know. I feel terrible.'

'You should. George is your friend.'

Midnight didn't have an answer to that.

'Come on,' said Koko firmly. 'We need to find Gabe.'

'Gabe!' called Koko. 'We have to help George!'

Gabe looked up from the fence he was mending, and wiped the sweat from his brow.

'Why?' asked Gabe, looking at Midnight. 'What's wrong with him?'

'Tell him,' said Koko.

Midnight gulped.

'I'm not your son.'

Gabe nodded patiently. 'I see. Whose son are you then?'

'A Black Russian Terrier called Bear. So was my mother. A Black Russian Terrier, that is. But she's called Jet.'

Gabe took a deep breath.

'Okay,' he said matter-of-factly.

'What do you mean, okay?' asked Midnight. 'I've lied to you!'

'I'm not going to tell you who to be any more, George,' replied Gabe. 'If you want to be a dog, be a dog. If I've learned anything in the last few days, it's that bottling up your thoughts and feelings doesn't work. Besides, if we can't dream a little when we're kids, when can we?'

'No!' cried Koko. 'You don't understand! He's a boy on the outside, but inside he really is a dog. The fountain's magic, Gabe. Think about it – you know it's true. Think of Gogmagog; the vegetable garden; that special feeling we all have living here. Once a year, at Midsummer, it has body-swap powers. That may be George's body, but inside, it's Midnight.'

'Midnight . . . as in Clive's Midnight?'

Midnight nodded. 'My master wants the fountain for himself, and he's prepared to sacrifice Lady Jane and Koko to get it. George tried to stop him . . . so . . . so . . .' Midnight was finding it difficult to get the words out. 'So Clive sent him to the dogs home. Unless we get him out, he could be stuck as a dog for ever and it's all my fault!'

It was a lot to take in, and Gabe's mind was whirring.

'I did wonder why George was eating so much. But come on – a body swap?'

'It's true,' said Midnight.

'Quick!' urged Koko. 'Ask him something only a dog would know!'

Gabe thought for a moment.

'Why do you guys eat grass?'

'Why do you eat salad?' said Midnight. 'Because it tastes good.'

'Okay,' said Gabe. 'Why do you chase your tail?'

'How else am I going to catch it?'

Gabe nodded. 'Last one. Why do you turn round and round before you do a poo?'

'I have absolutely no idea,' replied Midnight.

There was a short pause while Gabe considered Midnight's answers.

'I'm convinced,' said Gabe.

'You guys need to go, now!' urged Koko.

'But . . . what about you and Lady Jane?' asked Gabe. 'We need to warn her!'

'We'll be fine,' said Koko. 'We have to get George back, or he and Midnight will be stuck like this for ever!'

CHAPTER TWENTY-SIX

Georg woke with a start. Where was he? The smell of disinfectant was everywhere: on the rubber mat he was lying on, the plastic crate he had been sleeping in, the concrete floor of his kennel, and the blue mesh that walled him in.

Squeezing himself out of the crate, he stretched his back legs, and wandered up to the mesh. He was in what seemed to be a small courtyard, one side of which was lined with kennels; his was at the end of the row. It was late afternoon and the sun was low in the sky. He could hear the snoring and snuffling of a dozen dogs, their scents rippling in the breeze.

One scent was particularly ripe and as his eyes adjusted to the afternoon sunshine, he saw to his horror that the very next cage contained an enormous sleeping bulldog.

'Hey,' whispered a voice.

A sausage dog in the next-but-one kennel raised its head.

'Name's Frank. You just arrived, huh?'

'Yes,' signalled George, not wanting to wake the sleeping mound between them. 'That guy, Timmy—'

The bulldog stirred, and George fell silent.

'Gave you a sleeping pill,' finished Frank. 'He

does it to everyone. Total trickster.'

The bulldog licked its lips, leaving one giant tooth on display. George felt his chest tighten.

'How long was I out?' asked George.

'Like, the whole night and day.'

'No!' George gulped. 'I have to get out of here.'

'So what are you in for?' pressed Frank.

George paused, wondering how the swapping-bodies-with-a-dog story would go down. On reflection, he thought, maybe it was better to act tough.

'Biting,' replied George.

'Guilty?'

George panted.

'Were you provoked?'

George nodded and Frank shook his head in disapproval.

'Why do they do that? They provoke us; we bite.

And who carries the can? We do.'

The bulldog shifted its weight, but George's curiosity got the better of him.

'How about you? You sound like you're from—'

'Manhattan. Waterside Plaza. Originally, that is. But my family were living in London, next to a huge park. It was beautiful. Grass, trees. Everything you could want. We were very happy.'

'So what happened?'

'They forgot me.'

'What?'

'They forgot me. They took a trip; they stopped for gas. They forgot me.'

'You can't be serious?'

'It happens. They were diplomats, busy lives. I'd take them back tomorrow.'

For a moment, George was lost for words, and his tail twitched, unsure what signal to send.

'Your family left you behind, and you're not angry?'

'Are you kidding? If they came in here, looking for me . . . I'd be overjoyed. I'd lick them to death! Their ankles, anyway. I'm not the tallest dog you'll ever meet.'

'I don't understand,' said George, baffled.

'Sure you do,' urged Frank. 'Dogs don't hold grudges. Ask anyone in here. Hey, Daisy!'

To George's horror, Frank rattled the wall of the sleeping bulldog's cage. Daisy shook her muzzle, raised her head, and opened her saucer-like eyes.

How strong was the mesh between them? George really didn't want to find out.

'Meet, err . . .' Frank paused. 'Hey, new guy. What's your name?'

'Midnight,' squeaked George.

Daisy licked her nose.

'What would you do if you met your owners, Daze?'

'Tear them limb from limb,' growled the bulldog menacingly.

George felt his pulse quicken. But Daisy wagged her tail, and gave a friendly bow. She was joking!

'Once I'd rolled over and let them tickle my tummy!' she barked.

George closed his eyes and panted, enjoying the joke. Frank howled, and wagged his tail so fast it became a blur. A Jack Russell in a far-off kennel raised its head, ears twitching. 'That's funny!' he crowed. Soon all the dogs were panting, hooting and howling.

'Phew,' barked George to Daisy. 'I was worried you guys might be unfriendly.'

'Us?' barked Daisy in surprise. 'You don't want to worry about us.'

'We're the good guys,' piped Frank.

'It's the lifers you want to worry about,' grunted Daisy.

'The lifers?' barked George.

'The dangerous dogs. Soon as you're out of quarantine,' explained Frank, 'either you join us, or you join the lifers.'

'You join us,' added Daisy, 'you get adopted.'

'*Might* get adopted,' corrected Frank. 'You join the lifers, you're here for keeps.'

'Wait,' barked George. 'Back a bit: what's quarantine?'

'Nothing to it,' barked Frank. 'You just stay in your kennel.'

'For how long?'

Frank wasn't sure, so he turned to Daisy. 'How long, Daze?'

'I don't know.' Daisy shrugged. 'Ten days?'

'Ten days!' George's mouth went dry. 'I haven't got ten days!' The horror of his situation was beginning to dawn on him. Koko and Lady Jane were in danger, and he was locked up in a dogs home!

'Or of course you could escape,' added Daisy.

There was a pause. Had George misheard?

'Sorry,' barked George. 'Did you say *escape*?'

'Like Scruff,' chipped in Frank helpfully.

'Scruff was the dog who used to be in your kennel,' explained Daisy patiently. 'That's why it's empty. He found a tunnel.'

'Under that green plastic thing,' said Frank, pointing his nose in its direction. 'There's a storm drain down there. That's what Scruff said anyway.'

'Next day he was gone,' added Daisy.

But George wasn't really listening; he was already scratching at the green plastic drain cover in the corner of his kennel. Suddenly he uncovered a folding plastic handle that he could grip with his teeth. Closing his eyes, he pulled it with every ounce of strength he could muster.

The cover hinged open. Below it was a drain.

A big drain.

Big enough to take a big black shaggy dog!

CHAPTER TWENTY-SEVEN

George sniffed at the open drain, searching for clues as to what might be down there. Was it safe? The local rats seemed to think so, judging by how many of them had passed by that night. He sniffed again: centipedes; rotting leaves; stale rainwater. And again: slugs; empty drinks cartons; wet wipes. Amongst it all, he was sure he could pick out the fresh scent of a dog. Could that be Scruff?

A clanking sound jolted him back to reality. Timmy, the guy who had given him the sleeping tablet the night before, had entered the furthest kennel.

'Right, you horrible lot!' he yelled. 'Grub's up. And be quick about it; I've got tickets for a music festival!'

'What's going on?' hissed George.

'Feeding time,' answered Frank. 'If you want to do this, you better hurry.'

The sound of dog biscuits being poured into a metal bowl rang out across the yard. George's stomach played bass; he hadn't eaten since breakfast the previous day. But he didn't dare wait. He pushed back the drain cover with one of his hind legs, and backed down into the hole.

'Good luck!' barked Daisy.

'If you see my family, tell them where I am!' woofed Frank.

'I promise,' replied George, his head propping up the drain cover. 'See you on the outside!'

And with that, he ducked down into the darkness.

The pipe he found himself in wasn't quite big enough for him to stand up, and it was much more difficult to move than he could ever have guessed. Bit by bit, he began to crawl forward, resting now and then by lying flat and panting. It was pitch black, and he soon lost all track of time.

The journey was longer than he could ever have imagined. Just when he was starting to think he might spend the rest of his life not only as a dog, but as a dog trapped in a very narrow pipe underground, his nostrils locked on to the delicious whiff of fresh air! Scruff's scent was even stronger now, and he squirmed forward, determined to reach the exit . . .

His nose struck the end of the tunnel and, sniffing the grass-laden perfume of fresh air, heavy with pollens and particles of sun-baked earth, he found himself rearing up on his hind legs. His head struck something hard, which instantly gave way, and he found himself peering out of a green plastic drain cover, on to what appeared to be a wide grass playing field, his eyes dazzled by the evening sun.

'Quick!' barked a nearby voice. 'Before anyone sees you!'

As quickly as he could, George scrambled up into the light.

'Nice one!' barked a thin grey dog with grizzled fur, giving a quick play-bow, and then running around him in circles. 'You made the same mistake I did! I'm Scruff, by the way.'

'Mistake?' asked George.

'The storm drain!' barked Scruff, lying down flat in the grass, his ears forward and his tail swishing playfully. 'We both went up the slope instead of down!'

'What do you mean?' barked George, utterly confused.

'If you go down, it takes you to the river. But we went up!'

'I don't understand,' replied George. 'I thought we'd escaped?'

That was too much for Scruff, who collapsed into giggles, rolling helplessly on the grass.

'Escaped!' he echoed. 'Escaped?' he cackled. 'We're with the lifers!'

George's surroundings suddenly came into focus. The playing field was ringed by electric fencing: at one end was a row of open kennels, and at the other was some well-worn dog agility equipment. Lounging on top of it was a pack of the most terrifying dogs he had ever laid eyes on!

As he watched, a Staffordshire bull terrier raised its head and swivelled its one remaining ear towards him.

'Uh-oh,' barked Scruff.

'Who's that?' squeaked George.

'Winston,' answered Scruff. 'He's second in command.'

'Second?' repeated George, his stomach turning. 'Who's first?'

'The Top Dog,' said Scruff.

'And what's a Top Dog?' asked George, only half wanting to know.

'Trust me. No one messes with the Top Dog.'

As Scruff spoke, Winston slunk down off the A-frame ramp and trotted towards them.

'Okay. I'm not a dog,' explained George quickly.

'My name's George. I'm a human, and I did a body swap.'

'Seriously?' asked Scruff, sniffing at George to see if he was telling the truth.

'Seriously. That's why I came down the pipe. My humans are in danger and I need to get to them before midnight.'

'In that case,' replied Scruff wisely, 'I hope you win the fight.'

'What fight?' George licked his lips, but his tongue was dry.

Winston padded to a halt some distance away, his head tilted to one side, sniffing the air.

'The one you're about to have with Winston,' barked Scruff cheerily.

'Beat Winston, and you'll get to meet the Top Dog. And the Top Dog is the only one who can get you out of here.'

'And if I lose?' asked George.

'You know your problem?' countered Scruff. 'You think too much. Evening, Winston,' he barked. 'This is George. He came in through the out door, just like I did.'

'Is he challenging me?' growled Winston.

'One hundred per cent,' answered Scruff, before George could reply. 'And I'm the referee.'

'Referee?' replied Winston, with an expression of surprise. 'Since when do dog fights have referees?'

'I get it,' said Scruff. 'You don't want a fair fight; you might lose.'

'Did I say that?' barked Winston. 'Be my guest.'

'Very good,' announced Scruff. 'Would you please begin by walking around each other, sizing one another up?'

Winston began to circle George, his muscles

squirming beneath his sleek dark brown coat. George did his best to copy Winston's moves; he glanced at Scruff for reassurance, and received a subtle nod.

'Good,' barked Scruff. 'Would you please sniff noses . . .'

George and Winston touched muzzles. George learned two things about Winston: first, he had a healthy wet nose, and was therefore in peak physical condition; and second, he'd had chopped liver for breakfast.

'Great. And now bums.'

'Excuse me?' George had not been expecting that particular section of the routine.

'You circle each other; you touch noses; you sniff bums. It's the law,' replied Scruff gravely.

'I'm not sniffing his bum!' protested George.

Scruff leaned in towards George, so that only he

could hear. 'Do you want to meet the Top Dog, or not?' he asked in a hushed growl.

'Fine,' barked George, and stood still. 'Go ahead.' He tried to look as dignified as possible while he waited for Winston to finish sniffing.

'Your turn,' said Winston. George closed his eyes, wandered forward, and gave the air a cautious sniff.

'Closer,' urged Scruff. 'You're nowhere near.'

George flashed Scruff an irritated look, then closed his eyes once more and did as he was asked . . .

Scents exploded in the air around him: dazzling him with detail. Suddenly, he knew everything about Winston it was possible to know: the litter of seven he had been born into, and cast aside as the runt; catching his ear in a bicycle wheel as a young pup; the pain and sadness when his elderly owner died; all this, and the fact that he had *definitely* had chopped liver for breakfast.

'Wow,' said George, forgetting himself. 'I really understand why you guys do this now.'

Scruff was in full flow. 'A quick snort, please,' he instructed, 'to show you have no desire to hurt one another.'

Winston snorted, but George was confused. 'Wait . . .' He cocked his head to one side. 'We're not going to hurt each other?'

It was Winston's turn to look puzzled. 'Of course not,' he replied. 'What do you think we are, animals?'

'Best of three. And we're off!' howled Scruff.

Before George had time to think, Winston leaped into the air, closing his jaws around George's ear, pressing with just enough force so that George knew he had been bitten, but without wounding him in the slightest.

Right, thought George. *I need to watch those teeth.* But while he was thinking, Winston jumped again, striking George with his left paw, right on the tip of his nose!

The two of them broke apart, panting. George felt his insides deflate like a burst balloon. He'd lost! Best of three, and Winston had made two strikes!

'One—nil to Winston!' called Scruff.

George looked at Scruff in bafflement.

'You're bleeding a bit,' explained Scruff. 'And that's against the rules.'

George nudged his paw against his snout, and sniffed it; there was a tiny spot of fresh blood.

Winston snorted. 'Sorry,' he barked. 'I caught you with one of my claws.'

Once again, Scruff leaned in close, so only George could hear. 'Stop thinking,' he whispered, indicating

George's head with his paw. 'And start fighting,' he growled softly, pointing to George's heart.

Furious with himself, George snorted, leaped, and pressed his right paw against Winston's ear!

'One all!' called Scruff.

But George wasn't listening; in fact, he wasn't thinking at all. Instead, everything went into slow motion, as he began to dance, whirling round and round, just as he had seen Midnight do the very first time they met. Winston could only watch in confusion as George sailed past, tapping Winston on the back of the head with his rear left paw!

George landed hard on the ground, and everything sped up to real time.

For a moment, all three dogs stared at one another in silence.

'Two—one to George!' barked Scruff in utter surprise.

Winston bowed gracefully. 'Welcome to the pack,' he announced solemnly.

'Thank you,' George panted, trying to catch his breath. 'I don't suppose I could speak to the Top Dog now?'

Winston stood proud. 'Follow me,' he barked.

They approached the pack, and one by one the lounging dogs sat up to attention. Only one of them, an elderly Dalmatian, remained lying down, guarding the entrance to the A-frame.

'New dog wants to meet the Top Dog,' barked Winston.

'Not today he doesn't,' replied the Dalmatian. 'She's in one of her moods.'

'He's earned the right,' replied Winston. 'We fought; I lost.'

The Dalmatian raised itself to its feet reluctantly and stepped aside.

'It's your funeral, champ.'

George glanced at Scruff, took a deep breath, and stepped inside.

His first impression was that the A-frame was empty. Was the Top Dog a figment of everyone's imagination, or was Scruff playing a trick on him? Then, in the corner, he spotted a tiny mound of white fur.

'Excuse me?' barked George.

The mound didn't move.

George cleared his throat.

'Are you the err . . . the Top Dog? Because I really need your help.'

Still nothing.

'My humans are in danger and I have to get out of here.'

The lump uncurled and a pink nose came twitching towards George.

Two pink eyelids opened to reveal a pair of deep blue eyes.

George frowned as he recognized . . .

An albino chihuahua!

'Snowball!' he yelped. 'It's me, George!'

CHAPTER TWENTY-EIGHT

'George?' repeated Snowball suspiciously. 'That was my human's name. How do you know that? Who's after me?!'

'I thought I'd never see you again,' blurted George, drowning in a giant wave of surprise and delight. He wanted so badly to bound forward and greet her, but could see how unsure she was.

'I don't understand.' The hair on Snowball's back bristled.

'My mum got sick,' explained George tenderly. 'And we had to give you away.'

Snowball's head tilted in confusion. 'But . . .' she murmured. 'But . . .'

'I'm a dog,' finished George. 'Yes, I know. I'm under a spell – the place I live has some strange magic and I've swapped bodies.'

Snowball looked even more confused.

'Doesn't matter,' blurted George. 'I'm just so happy to see you!' His tail began to thump against the wall of the A-frame. 'I can't believe I've found you again!'

There was a long pause, while Snowball stared into George's eyes.

'George?' she barked softly. 'Is it really you?'

George felt his eyes flood with happy tears.

'Yes,' he signalled, pricking up his ears.

Snowball's tail began to wag, and she sprang

forward, licking his muzzle, his eyes, and his ears! George squirmed in delight, then rolled over on to his back, licking Snowball's chin as she leaped joyfully on to his chest. Soon they were both tumbling over and under each other, tails wagging, causing such a commotion that Winston poked his head into the den and gave a bark of alarm.

'What's going on?' he demanded. 'Snowball, are you okay?'

'No,' replied Snowball breathlessly. 'I'm not okay; I'm overjoyed. This is George, my human.'

'Your human?' asked Winston.

'I know what you're thinking,' replied George. 'I look like a dog. But inside I'm a human. Snowball's human. And now we've found each other again.'

'Did you ask?' barked Scruff, poking his head inside the A-frame and ruining the moment. 'About the escape? Nice den, by the way,' he added, glancing around. 'Love what you've done with the grass. Pulling it all up like that, to leave a cool patch of earth to lie in. Did you scratch the walls yourself?'

'Escape?' echoed Snowball, cutting Scruff short. 'George, what's going on?'

'I need your help,' admitted George. 'You remember my dad, Gabe, right?'

'I remember everything,' answered Snowball.

'What about Lady Jane and Koko?'

'Of course,' replied Snowball.

'Right. Well Lady Jane and Mr Yoshida, they got divorced. And the four of us . . . We're sort of like a family. Anyway, they're in trouble, and as pleased – no, delighted – as I am to find you, somehow I have to get out of here and get back to them.'

Snowball nodded wisely.

'I'll come back for you, I promise,' barked George.

Snowball panted.

'I'm here for life, George,' she barked softly. 'But I'll live happier knowing you're okay.'

She snapped to attention. 'Winston,' she announced. 'Set up the see-saw.'

'Seriously?' asked Winston. 'I thought that was only for emergencies?'

'And that's exactly what this is,' barked Snowball.

'Yes, ma'am!' Winston saluted, and vanished. A split second later, he reappeared. 'All hands on deck,' he muttered, and pulled Scruff after him.

George heard Winston bark instructions: there was the sound of multiple bodies climbing down off the A-frame; followed by something heavy being dragged across the grass; then the sound of multiple bodies climbing back up again.

'See-saw primed and ready for action,' announced Winston, poking his head into the den.

'Excuse me,' piped up Scruff, from over Winston's shoulder. 'I don't think anyone has looked at this from a health-and-safety viewpoint.'

George and Snowball touched muzzles.

'I don't want to leave you,' whispered George.

'You aren't leaving me,' replied Snowball. 'I'll always be with you, just like you're always with me.'

They stood in silence for a moment, then Snowball led George outside to find the entire pack perched on the roof. The see-saw had been dragged into a new position, and was now sitting between the A-frame and the barbed-wire-topped compound wall.

George understood the plan immediately.

'Thank you, brothers and sisters!' he barked, scrambling into place on the furthest end of the see-saw. There was a creaking sound as his end of the see-saw tipped to the ground, raising the end nearest the A-frame.

'On my count!' barked Winston. 'Three . . . two . . . one . . .'

'Geronimo!' howled Scruff, leaping too early. Unfortunately he was so light that he bounced straight off the other end of the see-saw and landed face down on the turf. 'Told you it wasn't safe,' he barked, bouncing straight back up. 'I one hundred per cent said that.'

'JUMP!' bellowed Winston, and the whole pack launched themselves off the A-frame, landing in acrobatic formation on the other end of the see-saw and catapulting George high into the air!

'JUMP!' bellowed Winston

CHAPTER TWENTY-NINE

George rocketed up towards the full moon!

Just when he felt he might leave Earth's gravity altogether, the ground appeared where the sky should be, and he realized that he was halfway through a stomach-churning backwards somersault. The barbed wire at the top of the compound wall fizzed dangerously close to the end of his nose then fell away, and he found himself staring up at the stars again as he plummeted backwards towards the ground!

His fall was broken by a large pile of empty cardboard boxes. He had landed in a skip on the other side of the wall!

'Thanks, guys!' he barked.

He heard a chorus of joyous replies!

There was no time for delay. He had to get to Hill House before the clock struck twelve!

Curiously, he seemed to know exactly which direction to travel in. As a boy, he knew automatically which way was up and which way was down; as a dog, he knew which way was home too. He trotted to get some speed up, then began to run, his tail swishing right and left and his ears flapping in the wind!

He sensed a short cut, and ducked under a hedge into a field full of sugar beet. After a quick glance to check the coast was clear, he raced across it, paws sinking in the soft earth, then scrambled under a low barbed-wire fence on the other side. Unfortunately his tail caught on one of the barbs, and as he turned to free it with his teeth a small vehicle came racing around the corner!

BEEEEEEEEEEP!

A familiar-looking electric buggy mounted a traffic island, smashed through a plastic bollard, and came screeching to a halt on the opposite side of the road.

It was Gabe! And Midnight was right beside him!

'*Dad?*' barked George. '*What are you doing here?*'

'George!' cried Gabe, leaping out of the driver's seat.

George sprang up and placed his paws on his dad's chest!

'Are you okay, son? Midnight told me everything,'

said Gabe, hugging him tight. 'I'm so sorry! I had no idea!'

'*Quick!*' barked George. '*We don't have much time!*'

'What do you mean?' asked Midnight.

'*Koko and Lady Jane are in danger!*' urged George. '*Clive's going to turn them into animals at midnight! We have to stop him!*'

'What's he say?' asked his dad.

'Clive tricked us!' shouted Midnight. 'We have to get back to Hill House!'

'*Dad, take the dual carriageway!*' barked George. '*And if we pass a policeman, make sure you're speeding!*'

'Gogmagog, Gogmagog, Gogmagog, Gogmagog!' chanted Clive, his hand stirring the fountain's surface.

Lady Jane and Koko were sitting back to back on fishing stools with their hands tied; beside them stood Clarence, holding the rabbit and the budgie in their cages.

'Let's all have a little drink, shall we?' Clive teased, filling a champagne glass from the fountain. 'To celebrate the brilliance of my plan. On second thoughts, maybe not all of us; Clarence and I aren't very thirsty.'

Lady Jane tried to speak, but like Koko, she had been gagged with one of Clive's many silk handkerchiefs.

'Lady Jane,' announced Clive. 'You have been trusting and defenceless, so it seems only right you should swap bodies with a rabbit.'

Like any good assistant, Clarence removed the rabbit from its cage right on cue.

'While you, Koko . . .' Clive's eyes narrowed.

'You have chirruped incessantly. There seems no animal more fitting to receive your soul than this irritating budgerigar . . .'

Koko also tried to speak; from her expression, whatever she was trying to say wasn't very polite.

Ignoring her, Clarence prepared the budgie for its starring role.

'Now then,' said Clive breezily, bringing the glass up to Lady Jane's lips. 'One drop. That's all it takes.'

Bright headlights swept across them as Gabe's buggy powered up on to the forecourt in a spray of gravel.

'It's over, Clive,' shouted Gabe.

'Says who?' crowed Clive, shielding his eyes.

'The police,' called Gabe. 'That's their siren.'

'They know all about the jewels!' bluffed Midnight.

Clive frowned, listening carefully. Sure enough, there it was – the sound of a squad car, its siren growing louder and louder!

Clive's eyes widened in alarm.

'Clarence!' he hissed. 'What time is it?'

Clarence checked his stolen pocket watch.

'Two minutes to twelve!'

Clive's eyes darted around in their sockets, as his brain worked overtime!

'Hands up, the pair of you!' ordered Gabe.

'There's no point running!' warned Midnight.

To prove the point, George bared his teeth and growled.

The squad car entered the forecourt, sirens blaring, and pulled to a dramatic halt. As the policeman climbed out, Clarence threw the holdall at Clive's feet and raised both hands.

'It was all Clive!' he squeaked. 'I had nothing to do with it!'

The policeman frowned.

'He's right!' hooted Clive, gulping from the glass. 'It was all me! Which is why I'm switching bodies with Clarence!' Before anyone could stop him, he poured the rest of the water into Clarence's mouth!

Or at least, he tried to. Clarence shook his head, refusing to open up.

'Drink!' threatened Clive. 'Clarence, drink!'

What George did next was pure instinct. He launched himself at Clive, his two front paws striking the magician right in the middle of the chest, knocking him backwards into the fountain!

Splosh!

Clive landed bottom-first in the water, his mouth a perfect oval of surprise!

For Gogmagog too, there was no time to think. He had been basking in the bulrushes, when his barbels sensed a familiar bitter taste: bitter, and yet somehow sweet, as it was the taste of his mortal enemy.

It took the work of a moment to shimmy his way over to where the water from the fountain met the lake; it took the genius of countless generations to open his mouth wide, and take a huge gulp!

CHAPTER THIRTY

Moonlight flashed bright on the surface of the water, and Clive's head lolled forward like a rag doll.

'Clive?' asked Clarence. 'Are you okay?'

But Clive was out for the count.

There was a pause while the policeman tried to make sense of what he'd just seen.

'Are you the owner of this dog, sir?' called the policeman to Gabe. 'Because he's out of control. Come to think of it . . .' He peered at George in disbelief. 'I think he waved at me yesterday.'

Instead of answering, Gabe rushed forward to untie Lady Jane, who threw herself into his arms. Midnight ignored his waterlogged master, and attended to Koko.

'Koko!' gasped Lady Jane. 'Are you all right?'

'Fine,' gulped Koko. 'You?'

'I'm so sorry, children,' said Lady Jane tearfully, wringing her hands. 'You were right, all of you. You said that Clive was up to something, and I should have believed you. In fact . . .' She took a deep breath. 'I should have believed myself. Right from the beginning, I felt something wasn't quite right. But the more I felt it, the more I tried to convince myself otherwise.'

GONG! GONG! GONG!

The clock in the hallway began to strike midnight.

'*Quick!*' barked George, jolting back to reality. '*We need to swap bodies!*'

'On it!' replied Midnight, rushing forward to haul Clive out of the fountain.

GONG, GONG, GONG!

'Does someone want to tell me what's going on?' asked the policeman.

GONG, GONG, GONG!

'Gogmagog, Gogmagog, Gogmagog, Gogmagog,' chanted Midnight, stirring the water.

The policeman frowned, turning to the fountain. 'Erm . . . Excuse me?'

But Midnight ignored him, placing a drop of enchanted water on George's pink tongue, and another on his own.

'Young man?' insisted the policeman. 'I'm talking to you.'

GONG, GONG, GO-O-ONG!

There was a blinding flash of moonlight, and by the time everyone's eyes had recovered, George and Midnight were fast asleep.

It was George that stirred first.

He sniffed through his nose. 'I can't smell anything!' he said joyfully. 'And I can see *everything*! Wait! I can talk!'

Midnight's nose twitched. Then he opened his eyes and barked excitedly.

'I know!' said George, understanding him perfectly. 'Me too, but the other way around!'

'George! Midnight!' exclaimed Koko, rushing to embrace her friends. 'You're back!'

Gabe and Lady Jane beamed at one another.

'Okay,' said the policeman to Gabe, his patience

stretched to its limit. 'I'm booking you for speeding.'

'Wait,' said George urgently. 'We were only speeding because we wanted you to chase us! This is Clive Blaise, the not-very-famous magician. And these –' he strode over to Clarence's holdall and removed the purple velvet bag – 'are the jewels he stole on his most recent cruise.'

'Jewels?' repeated the policeman, wondering if he had heard correctly.

'Including this diamond butterfly necklace,' explained George, producing it with a flourish.

'And this pocket watch,' added Clarence, guiltily.

The policeman's mouth fell open in surprise. His last case had involved a missing tractor tyre, and the thought

295

of catching an international jewel thief was more exciting than he could imagine. Pulling himself together, he turned to Clive and cleared his throat.

'Clive Blaise,' he began. 'You do not have to say anything, but it may harm your defence if you do not mention when questioned something you later rely on in court.'

Clive suddenly sat bolt upright. Something flickered in his eyes, and for a moment he looked like he was going to throw up. But all that came out was a single word.

'Gogmagog,' he croaked.

'Gogmagog,' croaked Clive

ONE MONTH LATER

'Where are they?' Koko sighed. She and Lady Jane were waiting for Gabe, George and Midnight to return from yet another visit to the dog pound.

'We have to be patient, Koko,' said Lady Jane. 'This has been a long and difficult process, you know that. And there's no guarantee they'll let Gabe take Snowball, even today. Everyone has to be sure it's the right way forward, for Snowball and for us.'

'I just hate thinking of her like that, locked up in there without her family.'

'It's a dogs home, Koko, not a prison,' said Lady Jane reassuringly. 'And a very good one at that.'

'Speaking of prisons,' said Koko. 'This arrived from Clarence.'

She held up a letter.

'He's really sorry, for all the trouble he caused us. And he's been to visit Clive.'

'What, in prison? How is he?'

'A bit under the weather, I think, from whatever bug he caught when he fell in the fountain. But he's eating well, particularly seafood.'

Out in the hall was the sound of voices.

'Sssh,' said Lady Jane. 'They're here.'

In rushed Midnight giving a series of barks.

George wasn't far behind. 'Guess who we've got?' he exclaimed.

'Here she is!' said Gabe, stepping into the sitting room. He had one arm tucked in his jacket, and as he drew it out, Snowball appeared, her pink nose sniffing in the morning sunlight.

'She's beautiful,' Lady Jane said with a smile.

There was more barking out in the hall.

'Oh yes,' said Gabe, with a twinkle in his eye. 'Sorry, Jane. I couldn't resist it.'

'Come on, you guys!' George beamed. He gave a short whistle, and in came trotting Frank . . . then Daisy . . . then Scruff!

'Do you want to explain this, Gabriel?' asked Lady Jane with mock severity.

'Not really,' said Gabe, setting Snowball down so she could greet her three friends.

'Though if we're desperate for space, maybe they could live in the cottage?'

'But where will we go?' asked George.

'Ah yes,' said Lady Jane, her eyes twinkling. 'Gabe . . . Perhaps this is a good moment?'

Gabe smiled. 'Jane and I were wondering how you two might feel about us moving in together?'

'Moving in where?' asked George, hardly daring to hope.

'Here?' asked Koko.

Gabe and Lady Jane looked at each other, then nodded, smiling.

George didn't know what to say – he and Koko just beamed.

Over in the corner, Snowball and Midnight sniffed one another, bumped noses, then scampered across the hall, down the steps, and out into the garden, closely followed by Frank, Daisy, and Scruff.

At the bottom of the lake, Clive stared blankly through fishy eyes. Maybe one day, someone would rediscover the magic powers of the Hill

House fountain, and try to do a body swap. When they did, he would be ready. But until then . . .

He might as well see if he could find a few worms for lunch.

A NOTE FROM
THE AUTHOR

I'd written three books before this one: *The Night I Met Father Christmas* is about Jackson, my eldest son; *The Boy Who Made the World Disappear* features my middle son, Harrison; *The Day I Fell into A Fairytale* stars my daughter, Lana. I wanted to write a fourth story, but much to my dismay, I discovered I'd run out of children! That's when I had the idea to write a story about our dog, Jet.

Sometimes I write in coffee shops; there's something about hubbub that helps me focus. One day there was a bit too much hubbub, even for me. Two giant black fluffy dogs had entered with seven little pups, each with a different coloured collar. They were a breed I'd never seen before. The adult dogs were as big as a person, with giant white teeth and huge pink tongues like slices of boiled ham, and the puppies looked like teddy bears.

The owner told me they were Black Russian Terriers. Raven, the mother, had just given birth and the other full-grown dog with her was her sister, Midnight. There had been thirteen puppies in Raven's litter, twice as many as she had been expecting! Six were spoken for, and these seven were looking for homes. I called my wife and asked her to come and meet us in the park straight away. One little puppy with a yellow collar came trotting forward and sat looking straight up at her.

Two years, eight pairs of perfectly good shoes, one treasured sofa cushion, and fifty kilogrammes later, Jet is our family dog. Thank you, Jet, for inspiring this story; you are the best family pet we could wish for. I still suspect you drive our car when we're away. I hope you don't mind, but I used your auntie's name instead of yours, because it made me think of magic, spells, and the full moon . . .

ACKNOWLEDGEMENTS

First thanks must go to my own litter, Jackson, Harrison, and Lana. I write these books in the hope that families will read them aloud; unfortunately, that means my own family often finds itself on a rather short lead while I try chapters out. Heartfelt thanks too to my wife, Jessica Parker, who often shouldered more than her fair share of the parenting burden while I chased a deadline, only to see me run off after another one as soon as I'd caught it.

Daniela Jaglenka Terrazzini's other-worldly drawings are the perfect companions for these stories. Her illustration of Clive Blaise being carted away in a police van is one of my all-time favourites; a giant carp seems to stare out through Clive's hooded eyes, but I have no idea how that can be possible. Might Daniela have her own *Book of Shadows*, open on a gold stand in her studio?

I count myself very lucky to work with Rachel Denwood's close-knit pack at Simon & Schuster Children's Books, led by fellow alpha Ali Dougal. Lucy Pearse's incorrigible playfulness and nose for a story make her the perfect editor. Treats are also due to Sorrel Packham and the

Design department, Veronica Lyons for the copyedit, and Sally Critchlow for the proofread. Laura Hough and Dani Wilson have rounded up a flock of sales, and Ian Lamb, Sarah Macmillan and Eve Wersocki-Morris have run a sure-footed marketing and publicity campaign.

On the subject of publicity, tummy rubs all round to my personal publicist Clair Dobbs, together with Laura Vincent, and Rosina Fielder at CLD Communications. You have hunted down so many great publicity opportunities, though I may never forgive you all for the Agility Course on *The Pet Show* . . .

Luigi Bonomi, my literary agent, is a breed apart. I have never been rescued from a snowdrift by a St. Bernard, but it can't feel that different to one of Luigi's timely phone calls; thanks too to Hannah Schofield, Clementine Gaisman and all at LBA Books. Writing sometimes means taking time out from acting, and I'm truly grateful to Samira Davies at Independent for championing my writing, as I am to her dedicated assistants Alice Burton and Geri Spicer.

Jet's breeders, Ian Daly and Zoe Roberts at Crucially Canine, have been an invaluable source of information on all things BRT; I'd also like to thank Jenny Cole at Noah's

Ark Rescue in Gloucester for taking the time and trouble to explain the inner workings of animal rescue centres at a time when it was impossible to visit in person. I had no idea how much we all owe to privately owned rescue centres and their volunteers for making sure no animal goes uncared for.

A big part of the inspiration for this book was Bernithan Court in Herefordshire, a rose-bricked William and Mary house with a legendary carp pit, Redmire, in its grounds. I'd like to thank the Richardson family for sharing that magical house with me and so many others. It may interest readers to know that a carp called Clarissa, captured at Redmire in 1952, held the record for the biggest carp caught in Britain for nearly three decades. She weighed roughly twenty kilogrammes and lived out her days at London Zoo.

CHRISTMAS DELIVERED
in Ben Miller's next
magical adventure . . .

THE CLASSIC ADVENTURE FROM BESTSELLING
BEN MILLER

DIARY
OF A
CHRISTMAS
ELF

CHRISTMAS MAGIC, DELIVERED!

Tuesday 21 October

Last night I dreamed I was a Christmas Elf. It was Christmas Day, and we were all at Father Christmas's lodge in the Arctic Hills, celebrating another successful year.

At one end of the room was a roaring fire, framed by garlands of holly, ivy and mistletoe; at the other sat Father Christmas, flanked by his Right-Hand and Left-Hand Elves.

And in between sat the rest of us: row after row

of red-faced Toymaking Elves, feasting, laughing and joking.

I was just tucking into my second turkey leg, when Father Christmas stood and tapped his glass with a spoon, to get our attention. We all fell silent.

'Dearest elves,' he said, sliding gracefully off his chair and on to his feet. Unfortunately he is quite short, so all we could see behind the table was his red velvet hat.

'Ah,' said Father Christmas thoughtfully.

Steinar, his Right-Hand Elf, and Ola, his Left-Hand Elf, helped him to stand on the seat of his chair. Father Christmas mopped his face with his handkerchief, collected himself, and resumed his speech.

'You have worked tirelessly all year, and I am quite overwhelmed with gratitude. On behalf of all the children of the world, thank you, thank you, thank you!'

We all clinked glasses and drank huge mouthfuls of the most delicious mead.

'Now I know what you're all wondering,' Father Christmas continued. 'Who can it be? Who is my Christmas Elf of the Year?'

The room filled with excited chatter.

'Well . . .'

An expectant hush descended.

'Without further delay . . .'

Everyone looked around the room.

'My Christmas Elf of the Year is . . .'

An elf on the far table let out a yelp of excitement.

'The one and only . . .'

Steinar, the Right-Hand Elf, cleared his throat, impatiently.

'. . . Tog!'

That was ME!! *I* was Christmas Elf of the Year!

The room burst into wild applause.

'Up you get . . .' said my mother.

But I couldn't seem to get up from the table! It was as if my bottom was glued to my seat.

'. . . Tog, get up! You're late!'

I opened my eyes. I wasn't in Father Christmas's house at all. I was in my bunk, in the tiny room I shared with my four younger brothers and sisters: Twig, Leaf, Plum and Pin. My mother was shaking me by the shoulder.

'Your father and I are off to work! You need to get the little ones to school!'

Which was when I remembered who I really am: an unemployed one-hundred-and-sixty-year-old loser elf who is still living with his parents.

ENTER A
WORLD OF WONDER
WITH CLASSIC ADVENTURE FROM BESTSELLING
BEN MILLER